MISTAKENLY MARRIED

VICTORINE E. LIESKE

Copyright © 2016 by Victorine E. Lieske.

All rights reserved. No part of this publication may be reproduced, distributed or transmitted in any form or by any means, including photocopying, recording, or other electronic or mechanical methods, without the prior written permission of the publisher, except in the case of brief quotations embodied in critical reviews and certain other noncommercial uses permitted by copyright law.

Victorine E. Lieske

PO Box 493

Scottsbluff, NE 69363

www.victorinelieske.com

Publisher's Note: This is a work of fiction. Names, characters, places, and incidents are a product of the author's imagination. Locales and public names are sometimes used for atmospheric purposes. Any resemblance to actual people, living or dead, or to businesses, companies, events, institutions, or locales is completely coincidental.

CHAPTER 1

Penny wrung her hands and walked to the back of the room. She opened the chapel door to peek outside for the fifteenth time in the last few minutes. William had to show up. He just had to. She turned and smiled at her family, seated in the cheap folding chairs at the front of the Chapel-O-Love. "I'm sure the traffic has held him up."

Her mother gave her a teary smile. Dad appeared to be trying not to say, "I told you this was a bad idea." At least her sister, Kimmy, smiled and gave her two thumbs up, showing her support. Her little brother, Clay, just fiddled with his cell phone and looked bored.

Where was William? He promised he would come. Tears blurred her vision and she blinked them away. Not now, in front of her family. She couldn't be the mess-up they all expected her to be. Not again. She took a shaky breath and steeled her nerves. He wouldn't let her down. She'd known him for too long.

Well, "known" was probably not the right word. They hadn't actually met before. But she'd been chatting with him online for over two years. They'd shared things some real life couples probably hadn't. She knew *him*, knew his soul. Even if all she'd ever seen was a blurry photo of him, she loved William with all her heart.

She probably shouldn't have committed to marrying William without even skyping, but he had some kind of camera phobia. How could she insist? Would his looks really make a difference anyway? She loved his heart, not his dark hair or strong jaw line. If he couldn't bring himself to get on camera, she needed to support him. She'd meet him face to face in a minute anyway.

"Mrs. William Tucker," she whispered, testing out the sound of it on her tongue. A shiver of anticipation shot up her spine. She'd already known there was something special about him a couple of years ago, when they first chatted online. They'd always had a connection. Their hearts were melded together. And now—well, where was he?

She'd splurged for a limousine driver to pick him up at the airport. Surely he'd arrive any minute. Traffic was probably bad with all the December holiday madness. She took another peek out at the nearly empty parking lot, willing the long black car to materialize.

~

Harrison Williams gripped his carry-on and stalked down the jetway, brushing past the slower passengers and trying not to scowl. This was the last thing he wanted to be doing, meeting some ridiculous socialite. But his brother was insistent, so he agreed to keep the peace. All he had to do was talk to her. Then he could leave and tell his brother it didn't work out.

The whole idea of marrying some upper class money grabber just to gain access to his trust fund made his stomach turn. But Trent did have a point. He'd never see a dime of his money if he didn't jump through his stepmother's hoops. A business arrangement. That's what his brother kept telling him it was. Just a simple agreement so both parties could benefit.

He slipped his hand in his pocket and fingered the piece of paper with the address, his nerves jangling. A part of him wondered if she would be tolerable. Maybe even likeable. A frown pulled his lips down. What was he thinking, he'd fall in love with the girl? He smoothed his suit jacket and continued down the walkway. No need to be entertaining foolish thoughts.

A driver stood by the glass doors, the name "Williams" printed on the white piece of paper he held.

Harrison stared at the man. Really? Trent hired a limousine? Who was this woman he was trying to impress? Harrison greeted the man.

"Right this way, sir."

He followed the driver, shaking his head at the lengths Trent was going through just to impress some spoiled little— Harrison stopped himself and shook his head. He really shouldn't be labeling her before even meeting her. He slid into the plush seat and waited for the driver to put his carry-on in the trunk.

As the car pulled out into traffic, Harrison took a deep breath. This could be interesting. Maybe she would be different from what he expected. Maybe he should go through with his brother's crazy plan. If she, what was her name? Ashley? Amanda? Something like that. Oh, well. She probably wasn't what he would want, anyway. If he did end up marrying her, it would only be a formality. He needed his trust fund money so he could move out and finally get out from under his stepmother's control.

He closed his eyes and laid his head back. If nothing else, at least he got to get away for a little while. His job in

L.A. wasn't exactly exciting, but his grandfather had started up the Harrison Williams Investment Group from scratch, and his father had run it until he fell ill. Now it was his turn. Expectations, and all that. It was what he'd been born to do.

The car slowed and Harrison's eyes snapped open. They couldn't be there already, could they? He peered out the window and his mouth went dry. Chapel-O-Love? What the...?

He pulled his cell from his pocket and stabbed his brother's name. The line rang three times before he answered.

"Very funny." Harrison tried not to yell.

"Hey, bro! Did you make it to Las Vegas?"

The driver came around the car and opened his door. Harrison waved him away. "Of course I did. I can't believe you did this. You're insane."

A pause came through on the other end of the phone. "You're not getting cold feet, are you? Come on. It's just a girl. All you have to do is meet her."

"Meet her? Are you joking? I never agreed to *this*." Harrison pointed to the chapel, even though his brother couldn't see, and ground his teeth. He should have expected his brother to pull something crazy on him.

Trent blew out a breath. "If you want the trust fund, you have to do this. She's signed a one-year contract. It's not a big deal. People marry for money all the time. All you have to do is pay her a hundred thousand. That's a lot less than a divorce settlement. And she'll get something else out of this, too. Her parents are pressuring her to marry someone of stature."

Harrison gripped the phone so hard he was surprised he didn't crush it. No more words came out.

The front door to the Chapel-O-Love opened, and a smiling bride waved at him. He broke out in a sweat, flashed a weak smile at her, and motioned that he was on the phone. She nodded, then ducked back inside.

His brother's voice came through over the buzzing in his ears. "Listen, don't screw this up for me. Do you know how long I searched for a girl willing to do this? You don't exactly have the best reputation. After leaving Carol at the altar—"

"I caught her in the confessional with the best man!"

Trent sighed. "Everyone goes to confession."

Heat burned Harrison's face. "That wasn't confession. That was what you do before you have to confess."

"Maybe she wanted to save time," Trent muttered.

"I'm hanging up." Harrison pressed the disconnect symbol and slipped his phone back in his pocket. The driver stood by the door, Harrison's bag beside him on the sidewalk. What a fine mess this was.

The chapel door opened again and the bride smiled wide and motioned for him to come in. He stared at her. She wasn't bad looking. In fact, she didn't look at all like the stuck-up socialite he'd imagined. That was a plus in her favor. Her high cheek bones and almond shaped eyes were quite attractive. Her strawberry blonde hair was pulled back in a simple style, a cheap looking veil pinned to her head. She looked to be in her late twenties, which wasn't too much younger than him. The dress didn't exactly fit, but from what he could tell she was in shape.

Wait, was he really thinking he would go through with this? He must be insane. This whole idea was certifiable. But he'd spoken to five different attorneys who all told him the same thing. His father left his stepmother in charge of the trust funds. There was no legal way to take the money away from her, no matter what his father's intentions had been. He had to please her, and she wanted him married.

He let out a breath and climbed out of the limousine. His brother had set this all up, and already had a contract signed with this woman. All he had to do was walk inside and say, "I do."

The woman waved her arms. "Are you coming? We've got to hurry, or they're gonna charge us double."

He shrugged. Why not? It was only a year. Highly worth it for fifteen million.

∼

Penny stared at the man walking down the aisle. He was so handsome! She knew he would be. The photo he'd sent her was small, out of focus, and it was hard to tell what he looked like. Dark hair and chiseled features. But seeing him in person gave her a thrill. It was all she could do not to scream and jump around like she'd won the lottery. The closer he got, the more gorgeous he became. Her heart thundered in her chest. This was the man she'd bared her soul to. This was the man who understood her hopes and dreams.

And he was smokin' hot!

William stepped up to the altar and faced her. He looked a little nervous. Or mad. Why was he scowling like that? She leaned over. "You okay?"

He nodded and straightened his back. "Yes. Let's just get this over with."

Over with? Her heart sank. Why did he say that? She tried to keep the hurt from her face. "You sound like you don't want to do this."

His features smoothed. "I'm sorry. I do."

Maybe he was simply the nervous type. He did say he was shy around people. He probably struggled with social anxiety. That must be it.

She gave him a bright smile. "Me, too."

The minister said a few things. She didn't pay a lot of

attention because her soon-to-be husband smelled really good, and it distracted her. She detected a musky cologne and something else. Maybe cinnamon? She should be listening. This was her wedding.

She tore her eyes away from William and looked up to the minister. He was staring at her with an expectant look. Then he cleared his throat, and her cheeks burned. "I do!" she blurted, hoping it was what he wanted. He must have skipped to the vow part, since they were running late.

The minister handed them the little metal rings she'd purchased with the deluxe package. "You may exchange the rings," he said with a grand gesture.

William took her hand and slid the ring on her finger. Tiny zaps of electricity zinged through her, and her knees went weak. Holy cow, she'd married the right man.

"Now, you may kiss the bride."

William leaned over and pressed his lips to hers so quickly she almost missed it. Really? That was their first kiss? Disappointment flitted over her, but she pushed it away. He probably didn't want to give her a proper kiss in front of her family. They'd make up for it later.

After the rushed ceremony, her mother took a few snapshots. Her family stood and surrounded them. Her mother dabbed at her eyes. "Congratulations! I'm so happy to finally meet you. I'm Marci." When she pulled him into a hug, poor William looked stunned. Penny held in a giggle. Her mom could be a little overwhelming.

Her father patted her new husband on the back. "Welcome to the family." Then he leaned over and whispered quite loudly, "You'd better not break her heart."

Heat seared Penny's face. William's eyes grew wide, and his eyebrows rose. "Daddy. Stop teasing." She took her husband's arm. "This is my father, Arthur, my brother, Clay, and my little sis, Kim."

The minister cleared his throat. "I'm sorry, we have another couple scheduled in a few minutes. We'll need to hurry this along. The paperwork still needs to be signed."

Her mother wrapped her arms around Penny in a warm embrace. "I guess this is it. We'll see you for Christmas, right? It's only a couple of weeks away."

Penny nodded. "Of course, Mom."

"Have a wonderful honeymoon." Her mother took another quick photo before waving and following the family out. The minister ushered her and William to the back room.

∼

Harrison wasn't sure what he'd gotten himself into. Everyone was acting peculiar. If this girl came from privileged means, they didn't live like it. Her father's purple polyester suit looked like it had been hanging in the back of his closet for thirty years.

His thoughts were interrupted when the girl shoved a paper at him. He stared at her name. Penelope Marie Ackerman. A stately name. His stepmother would like it.

But they'd gotten his name wrong. How embarrassing.

Penelope grinned at him. "Let me get changed out of this dress, and then we'll head out." She disappeared into the back changing room.

After she left, he took the paper to the woman behind the desk. "They've typed my name in wrong. Can you re-do these, please?"

The woman took the sheet and nodded. After she typed up a new form, she held it out to him. "You'll need to take this marriage license to the bureau and show your driver's licenses. And there's a fee."

"That's fine." He took the form and stuffed it in his pocket. He loosened his tie and tried to shake the feeling something was wrong with the situation. This was what needed to happen, right? In order to get his stepmother off his back and fulfill the terms she had added to his trust fund. He stared at the cheesy photos of happy couples on the wall, most of them probably plastered.

A minute later, Penelope emerged wearing jeans and a T-shirt with the words, "Dear Math, I'm not a therapist. Solve your own problems," splayed across her chest. "Ready?" She picked up his carry-on and headed for the parking lot.

He trailed after her like a lost puppy. His head spun. What was going to happen now? Was he to go with her? What had his brother gotten him into? She stopped at a bright orange 1978 Pacer and dug in her purse, pulling out a set of keys.

"*That's* your car?"

Penny frowned, obviously displeased. "Shh. She's sensitive." She motioned to him. "Get in. It's unlocked."

"Of course it is," he muttered. "Who would steal this?"

Penelope either didn't hear him, or ignored the comment. She turned to him with a bright smile. "After we file with the bureau, we can swing by my apartment and grab my stuff. Then we can head out."

He was afraid to ask, but the words came out anyway. "Go where?"

Her light laughter filled the car. "To our honeymoon, of course."

She sped along the streets and before long Harrison found himself gripping the seat. Dear heavens, she drove like a mad woman. Her car smelled of cheap fast food. He felt like he'd entered some alternate universe.

The marriage bureau had them in and out faster than Penny's driving. No blood test. In a matter of minutes they were on their way.

Penelope drove like her life depended on it. How they didn't get in an accident, he didn't know. The car squealed to a stop in front of a small apartment complex. "I'll be right back." She hopped out and ran up the steps. The apartment door she stopped at had a neon pink paper taped to it. It looked like Penny's key wasn't working. She pounded on the door and yanked on the knob.

Harrison got out of the car. "Everything okay?"

Penny kicked the door. "No. I'm locked out!"

A balding overweight man came out of the management office, hitching up his pants.

Penny ran to the railing and called to him. "Theodore? What did you do?"

The man grunted. "I'm evicting you. You gotta pay the rent to live here, lady."

Harrison rubbed his temples. If Trent thought this woman was privileged, he'd been taken for a ride. No matter. He didn't care if his fake wife had money or stature. He only wanted to prove to his stepmother that he was legally married. The end. Penelope would do as well as anyone. She was probably happy to sign the contract and get the hundred grand.

"I was going to...I still had..." Penny looked like she was going to cry.

He had to do something. "Can she at least go in and get her stuff?" He started up the stairs.

Theodore took his time getting to the apartment. "I'll let you in." The keys jangled as he unlocked the door.

Penny huffed and pushed past him, Harrison following. She disappeared into a back room. The apartment was filled with threadbare furniture, surely pieces she found sitting near dumpsters. The floor was covered with green shag carpet from the seventies. The only light in the room came from a tacky Elvis lamp sitting on an end table.

Penny came out of her bedroom dragging an old suitcase stuffed so full of clothes it wasn't zipped all the way.

"You okay?"

She shook her head, tears springing to her eyes. "I thought I had another week. I thought we could—you could…" She burst into tears.

He reached down and took the suitcase from her. Unsure of what else to do, he pulled her into a one-armed hug. Then he said the lamest thing in the history of language. "There, there."

She hiccupped and wiped at her eyes. "None of my furniture will fit in my car."

"Come on. Let's go. I'll buy you new furniture."

"I have to bring Elvis." She picked up the lamp.

Sure. Elvis. Who couldn't live without a tacky Elvis lamp? He held in a smart remark. "Okay, then." He ushered her out the door.

They stuffed the suitcase and the lamp in the trunk and got in the car. She seemed to calm down as she drove. When they got to a red light, a high pitched voice sounded from her purse. "Text message! You have a text message!" Penelope fumbled for her phone, blushing. "Sorry. I hardly ever get a text, unless it's from you, of course."

Confusion clouded his brain. What was she talking about?

She stared at her phone. "Wait. It *is* from you. Did you text me while I was…" her voice trailed off as she stared at the device in her hand. The color drained from her face, and she looked up at him, horror filling her eyes. "William just texted. Says he's delayed." She swallowed, her lips trembling. "So if he's delayed, who are you?"

CHAPTER 2

Harrison wasn't sure what Penelope was talking about. "Haven't you been speaking to my brother, Trent?"

The light turned green and Penelope drove around the corner onto a residential street. She slammed on the brakes and hopped out of the car. He didn't know what else to do, so he stepped out as well.

She paced in the middle of the street, her hands fisted in her hair. "No, this can't be happening. I did *not* just marry a total stranger." She continued to pace and mumble.

"Stop! What are you talking about?" How had the situation careened out of control? It was like he was in a bad episode of the Twilight Zone. Did she say she'd married a stranger? Hadn't that been the plan?

She whirled to face him, pointing an accusing finger. "You! You ruined my wedding! Who are you, anyway? Some sicko who walks into other people's weddings and takes the place of the groom? Why would you do that? What could you possibly gain from—" Her eyes narrowed and she took a step toward him, her hands clenched into tight fists. "Are you a con artist?"

He held in a laugh. "Yes. I'm a con artist. I planned this whole thing to get your Elvis lamp." Harrison smirked, but took a step back onto the sidewalk in case she was the type to take a swing at someone. She looked a little unstable. And for heaven's sake, how could he have mistaken *her* for the woman Trent had sent him to meet? He should have asked for more details. How could he have just assumed? What a nightmare.

Her cheeks blushed pink, which looked rather cute on her, even though she was a nutcase. She drew nearer, stepping out of the street onto the grass. "Who are you?"

"Harrison Williams. And I didn't ruin your wedding on purpose. The driver at the airport had my name on the card."

The woman stomped and let out an exasperated grunt. "I told him 'William' not 'Williams.' How could he have messed that up?"

A kid on a bike whizzed by, and Harrison stepped to the side. "This was all just a horrible mistake. I flew into town today to meet a woman my brother set me up with."

Her nostrils flared and her eyes narrowed. "And it seemed perfectly natural to marry someone on a blind date?"

"It wasn't a normal blind date. It's more of an arranged marriage type of thing. A business transaction." As the words left his mouth, he knew how ridiculous they sounded. Who did that kind of thing? But what about her? "Surely you should have recognized that I wasn't your fiancé."

Her blush darkened. "William and I love each other. Just because we haven't met, doesn't mean we don't know each other's souls."

A laugh burst forth from Harrison, and not some polite chuckle either. A belly laugh so loud one of the neighbors moved the curtain to peek outside at him. "Let me guess, you met him on the Internet."

Penelope worked her jaw, her fists clenching and unclenching. No words came out.

"You—you don't even know—what he looks like?" he said between fits of laughter. Oh, this was rich.

She stared at him for a moment, but when she did speak, her voice was low and fierce. "At least I know my William. You don't even know who you're marrying. A business arrangement? What does that even mean?" She turned around and grunted in disgust. "Get in the car. We're going back to undo this mess."

"That's the first sane thing I've heard you say, Penelope."

"It's Penny!"

Harrison got in and slammed his door, then the crazy lady stomped on the gas and they took off.

⁓

"What do you mean, you can't tear it up?" Panic rose in Penny's chest and she tried not to hyperventilate. This could not be happening. "William's only been delayed. He could be here any minute!" She wanted to rip off the cheap metal ring and stuff it down his throat.

The minister tugged at his collar. "I'm sorry. Looks like you already filed the paperwork with the state. You two are legally married. But my brother's a lawyer. Has a place up the street. Jacobson, Smith and Talbott. They do annulments for real cheap."

She'd scraped the bottom of her bank account for the hundred bucks to get the deluxe wedding package and the fifty to pay the limo driver. And now she had to pay for an annulment so she could do the whole thing over again when William got there? She blew her hair out of her face in frustration. Maybe her father was right. Her life was one screw-up after another.

"How cheap?" Harrison folded his arms across his broad chest and Penny forced herself to look away. Dang. Why couldn't he have been William?

"Only four hundred dollars. A real bargain."

Penny about swallowed her tongue. "*That's* what you call cheap? I don't have that kind of money! This is some racket you guys have." She stormed out of the back room and into the chapel. Unfortunately she ran into a bride having her photo taken. The two went down in a tangle of white satin and lace. "Oh! Sorry."

The bride was too shocked to say anything, her mouth hanging open like she was a cod fish. Penny jumped up and helped her to her feet. "Just be sure you're marrying the right guy. It's four hundred bucks to get an annulment."

It wasn't until then that she noticed the chapel full of people. All eyes were on her. She pasted on a smile. "I mean, have a great wedding."

Penny turned and ran back into the office. Harrison was still talking to the minister. "How long will all this take?"

He cast a nervous glance at Penny. "One to two weeks."

"Are you crazy? My fiancé will be here any minute!" Of course, at that moment her phone screeched "Text Message!" and heat rose to her face.

She pulled out her cell and stared at the screen.

Sorry, my love, I cannot make it to Las Vegas today. I do apologize. Something has come up that cannot be avoided. Please don't hate me. Come meet me in Santa Barbara, and we will still have our honeymoon.

Her vision blurred as tears filled her eyes. William wasn't coming to marry her. She was being stood up at her own stupid wedding. But worse than that, he wanted her to go away with him—like some cheap fling. She hated the thought of a one-night stand. How many times had she told him she was holding out for a lifetime commitment?

Harrison stepped close. "What happened?" he whispered, his voice consoling.

She hadn't realized she was crying until then. "He's not coming." She choked on the words, then buried her face in his shoulder.

"Hush, now. It's not so bad. We'll get this all sorted out."

She clung to him in a desperate attempt to find something solid in her life of turmoil. She had no place to live. No job. No money. And now, no knight in shining armor to swoop in and carry her off into the sunset. All she had was a suitcase full of clothes, a beat-up old car, a man she'd mistakenly married, and her Elvis lamp.

Her day couldn't get any worse.

~

*H*arrison felt sorry for the girl. Sure, she was crazier than old Aunt Edna who ran around the house naked at night, but her sobs were affecting him. She loved this guy William. At least, she thought she did. And he had left her at the altar holding a cheap bouquet of plastic flowers. What a jerk.

Hating to see her cry, he patted her back. "Come on. Let's go. We can file the paperwork for the annulment and all this will be over soon."

She looked up at him with her red-rimmed eyes, mascara streaking down her cheeks. The minister handed him a box of tissues and excused himself. Penny pulled a few out and blew her nose. "I don't know what to do. Will and I were going to make a life together."

"You're better off without him."

The look she gave him said those hadn't been the right words to say.

"I mean, you can do so much better."

She stared past him, her face blank. Maybe she was in shock.

He wrapped his arm around her shoulders and guided her out the back door and around to the parking lot. "You'll be okay."

They stopped at her car. "You drive." She pulled out the keys and handed them to him. "I don't even know where we're going."

Harrison didn't really want to be seen driving a bright orange Pacer, but he nodded anyway. Now wasn't the time to argue. He opened the passenger door for her and helped her in. She looked like a deflated balloon. Lifeless. Flat.

He slid into the driver's seat. "I'll keep my promise. After we file, I'll buy you some new furniture."

"A lot of good it will do me. I have no apartment, if you remember." She stared out the window.

"I'll help you find one."

She shook her head. "The show I was in was cancelled, and then I was even fired from the coffee shop last month. Haven't been able to find anything else around here. I was hoping to find something out in California after William and I—" Tears pooled in her eyes and she quit talking.

Not again. He had to get her to stop crying. "Don't think about him. You need to concentrate on something more positive." Harrison pulled out of the parking lot, unsure of what that could be. Her life seemed rather dreadful.

Then it hit him. He was about to get an annulment in order to go meet a woman to convince her to marry him for a hundred thousand dollars. He glanced at Penny, the woman he was already married to. She could definitely use some cash.

And maybe she would do it for half.

"I have an idea."

Her hollow eyes didn't leave the window. "What?"

"Let's not annul this marriage."

"Ha, ha. Very funny." Not even a hint of a smile played on her lips.

"I'm serious. I'm here because I need a wife in order to get to my trust fund. You could use some cash. Why don't we stay married long enough to convince my stepmother that I've fulfilled her wishes? Then I'll give you fifty thousand dollars and we'll part ways."

"Yeah, right. Like you have fifty thousand dollars." She turned to glare at him, but when she saw his face, she blinked. "You're serious? You'd give me fifty thousand dollars to be your wife?"

"You're already my wife." He grinned at her.

"You're crazy. This whole thing was a mistake. We can't stay married." She waved the idea off like a pesky fly.

"You'd turn down fifty thousand dollars when you have no job, no place to stay, and only the clothes on your back, and you call *me* crazy?"

She pointed to the trunk. "You forgot my portable closet."

"Oh, that's right. And your lamp. You'll be fine, then. Elvis will take care of you." He smirked, pulling into the parking lot of Jacobson, Smith and Talbott.

Penny tossed him a grim smile before she turned serious. She sat for a few seconds in silence. "What would I have to do?"

"Just—"

"Wait! No, I can't. What am I thinking? Marrying a stranger? For money? I can't." She bit her bottom lip. "What about my family?"

He swallowed, unsure of what she meant. "What about them?"

"They think I'm a total flake. If they find out what happened, I will be the butt of every joke for eternity." She covered her face with her hands, and mumbled through her fingers. "I can't go home this Christmas without you or they'll know what a mess-up I really am."

"Then I'll go home with you. I can pretend to be William."

"What?" She peeked at him. "You'd do that?"

"Sure." How hard could that be? He pushed down the feeling that he was getting himself into trouble. "No problem."

Penny ran her hands through her hair. She grimaced and looked like she was trying to make some huge life decision. Finally she exhaled. "I can't. I'm always doing things like this, and I regret it later on."

Harrison tightened his grip on the steering wheel. He thought he'd convinced her. Maybe she needed a little more coaxing. "What can go wrong? It's not forever. It's only for a little while. No one has to know about this."

Indecision played across her face. "I don't know. It's crazy."

"Yes. But it could work."

She narrowed her eyes at him. "We'd be married just on paper, right? No sleeping in the same bed or anything?"

"Of course. What do you think I am?" He almost had her, he could tell. "Come on. Your family will love me. I promise. And I'll be the perfect gentleman. Cross my heart." He made the symbol over his chest.

She sighed again. "Okay."

"Okay, you'll stay married to me?" This was the weirdest conversation he'd ever had.

"Yes." A smile lifted one side of her mouth. "Let's blow this joint."

CHAPTER 3

Harrison pulled the Pacer into the restaurant parking lot and stared at the sign. "Are you sure you want to eat here?"

Penny punched his arm. "Come on, they have great food. Don't be a snob."

He exhaled, got out of the car, and followed Penny into Lord of the Onion Rings. They were in Las Vegas, for crying out loud, and *this* was where she wanted to eat? She was definitely different from all the other girls he'd gone out with.

He stepped around a cardboard cutout of some blond dude with pointy ears to get a better look at the menu. "What's on a Gandalf Burger?"

The freckled teen behind the counter looked bored. "Cheese, Pickles, Onions, Lettuce, and Mustard."

Penny tugged on his arm. "The Gollum burger is better. It's got bacon."

Sure. Why not. He shrugged. "Okay. I'll have the Gollum burger, a side of Precious Rings, and a Wraith shake."

The kid punched in his order and Penny grinned. "I'll have the same. That's my usual."

They waited for the food, and Harrison wished he'd changed into his casual clothes. He felt out of place wearing a suit. She didn't seem to notice. When the food came, Penny took the tray and led them to a booth in the corner.

He sat down and nodded to the two figures on the table. "What's with the little boy blue salt and pepper shakers?"

She laughed, a sound he was beginning to like. "That's Frodo and Samwise. You're not a big Tolkien fan, are you?"

"It's a little geeky, don't you think?"

"You caught me. Closet geek here." Her grin took over her whole face, like she smiled with all she had. How did she do that? She had an energy coming from within her. It was appealing.

"Text Message," screamed her purse. She pulled her phone out, pressed her lips together in a thin line, and punched in a return message.

"William?" he asked.

Penny nodded, her expression guarded.

He picked up his hamburger and took a bite, surprised that it tasted so good.

She texted back and forth with William as they ate.

Curiosity flickered inside him, and he tried to see what she was saying but the phone was always at the wrong angle. When he couldn't stand it anymore, he gave in. "What are you telling him?" He took a swig of his shake.

She smirked. "That when he didn't show up, I married someone else."

He'd witnessed a lot of spit-takes in his life, but had never performed one before. Chocolate shake spewed forth from his mouth, landing on her T-shirt. "You what?"

She grabbed a napkin and dabbed at her chest, a satisfied smile on her lips. He pulled several more from the dispenser and shoved them at her. "Sorry."

"He doesn't believe me."

"Who would? The whole thing's ludicrous."

She picked up her phone, typed one last message, and then shut the ringer off. "Well, it's over. I told him to put on a red shirt, because he's dead to me."

"What does a red shirt have to do with…" Harrison shook his head. "Never mind. I'm glad you told him off."

Penny stood and gathered their trash. "I still can't believe he didn't come. I mean, we've been chatting for two years. You'd think I'd know someone after all we've shared. He made me believe he wanted to get married." She blinked, obviously trying not to cry.

He bit back the words he wanted to say. Things like, 'How can you trust a random guy from the Internet?' and 'Maybe he's seven hundred pounds and they couldn't get him through the airplane door.' Instead, he put a sympathetic hand on her shoulder and said, "I'm sorry it didn't work out."

They got back in the car and looked at each other awkwardly. Harrison cleared his throat. "I guess we'll get a hotel tonight. We can book a flight for tomorrow, so you can meet my stepmother."

"Okay. Where does she live?"

"We live in Bel Air."

She raised an eyebrow. "*We?* You still live with your mother?"

He frowned, not wanting to tell her the reason he hadn't moved out yet. "Stepmother. And it's a twenty thousand square foot home. We barely see each other."

She slowly nodded. "I see." She pulled out of the parking lot and gunned it. "I'll find us a hotel." Ten minutes later she pulled into a Budget Inn, a red sign flashing 'vacancy.' She maneuvered the car around a broken beer bottle and pulled up to the front doors.

Harrison grimaced. "Surely Las Vegas has better hotels. Can't we stay somewhere a little less…ghetto?"

She huffed and flung her hand in the air. "Fine. It's your money. Get on your phone and find a place."

"Great idea." He had a five star hotel booked in a matter of minutes. The valet parking attendant raised his eyebrows at the Pacer, but didn't say anything. Harrison gave him a fifty. He checked in while the porter struggled with Penny's suitcase. After they were in their suite, he let out a breath and rolled his shoulders. "Much better."

He took in the plush accommodations. Large picture windows took up one wall, the view overlooking the beautiful lights on the strip. Two couches, a coffee table, fireplace and television made the living area cozy.

Penny grinned. "Nice." She walked into the bedroom and plopped down on the king sized bed and moaned. "Oh, this is *so* comfortable."

He frowned. Yes, he'd known it would be comfortable. And he was looking forward to it, after the day he'd had. But all the two and three bedroom suites were booked, and he couldn't be a jerk and make her sleep on the couch. He sighed. "Yep. I'll take the couch."

His cell phone rang, and he wasn't surprised to see Trent's name on the display. "Hey."

"Abby called." Trent's voice was pinched with annoyance. "You never showed up."

"Sorry. I made other arrangements." Harrison loosened his tie and took off his shoes.

"What's wrong with you? You can only burn so many bridges before—"

"I got married." He peeked into the other room to see if Penny was listening.

"You what?" Trent's voice squeaked. "Are you crazy? Who did you marry?"

"That's not important. I'm married now, and that fulfills the terms of the trust. I'm coming home with my wife and a copy of the marriage license." The other end of the line was silent. Harrison sighed. "Trent?"

"You're serious?"

"Of course I'm serious." He stood and crossed the room to give more space between him and possible listening ears. "You're the one who told me to marry as a business arrangement."

"Well, yeah, but not just anyone, for heaven's sake. Do you know the problems that could arise from your rash decision?"

Frustration welled in Harrison. "Yes, I know. But in my defense, at the time I thought you had set this entire thing up and already had a contract signed with her. But I don't think it will be an issue. She's agreed to help me out for fifty thousand. Getting her to sign a contract should be easy."

A pause carried more silence through the line. "Does she know how much you're worth?"

"Of course not."

"But she knows your name. She could Google you."

He rubbed the back of his neck. "I guess."

"And you guys didn't sign a pre-nup?"

Harrison's mouth went dry. "Um, no."

"You're screwed, Bro."

~

Penny sprawled across the bed and listened to Harrison talking. What was he saying? Something about getting her to sign a contract? She shrugged. If he was going to spend Christmas at her mom's house and pretend to be William, she'd sign anything he wanted. She really didn't care about anything else, not even the fifty thousand. Well, not much.

Sure, the money would save her, but it wasn't the real

reason she'd agreed to do this. The last thing she wanted to do was to go home alone, in shame. Her family already thought she was an airhead. Admitting to them that William was a cad and she'd somehow managed to marry a total stranger? No. That would be too humiliating. This way, her family could think she was happily married—for at least a little while. Later on she could tell them they'd had to end it. Being divorced at twenty-five was way better than telling them what really happened.

Besides, Harrison was a total hunk. Marrying him might prove to be just the distraction she needed to get over William. Even though she didn't want to admit it, she had fallen for William. He'd sympathized with her when she was down. He'd told her she was beautiful on the inside, where it mattered. As it turned out, all this time, he was just a jerk. Her chest felt hollow. Empty.

She dragged her suitcase into the spacious bathroom and slipped on a pair of sweats and a comfortable T-shirt. After brushing her teeth, she hopped into bed and picked up her cell phone. Before she knew what she was doing, she found herself reading one of her old text conversations from over a year ago.

P: Stink. What a totally no-good rotten day.

W: Why?

P: Arg. I got kicked out of school.

W: What?!? How do u get kicked out of belly dancing school?

P: Funny. Getting into the College of Performing Arts was my dream. And now everything's ruined.

W: What happened?

P: It wasn't my fault.

W: Of course not. What happened?

P: I may have insulted my interpretive dance teacher.

W: Y did u do that?

P: She called me inept! In front of the whole class.

W: How rude.

P: Yeah, I know. I didn't even mean to bump into Jenna.

W: Well, that doesn't sound that bad. Maybe u can apologize and get back in.

P: Hmm. Yeah, well, probably not after the fire.

W: The fire?!?

P: How was I to know that the next class was rehearsing for a stage production of Phantom of the Opera?

W: ?

P: There's this part where the stage erupts in flame. Bumping into Jenna threw me off balance. I grabbed a lever to steady myself and accidentally set the stage on fire.

W: What?! Was anyone hurt?

P: No. They were all over by the trap door making sure the teacher was okay.

W: Trap door?

P: Yeah, I had no idea that was what that button was for.

W: Oops.

P: So now they want me to pay damages, and I'm kicked out of the school, and my dad is gonna FREAK.

W: I'm sorry, sweetie. What can I do to make it better?

P: Nothing. I just needed to vent. Thx for listening.

W: Anytime. I'm here 4 u.

P: I don't know what I'd do without you.

W: Don't get discouraged. You're amazing. U know that, right? I love u.

Penny stared at the screen, the words blurring together. It was the first time he'd said he loved her. Pain rippled through her chest, and a tear slid down her cheek. It was stupid, but she loved him. She knew she was being silly. Who falls in love with someone they've never met? Of course it was ridiculous.

But he was always there for her. Would always bring her

up when she was down. She told him everything, and he loved her just the same. Her heart ached for him.

She wiped the tears from her face and tossed the phone on the night stand. She needed to get a hold of herself. He was not who she thought he was, that was apparent.

She needed to move on.

CHAPTER 4

Harrison blinked against the bright sunlight coming through the sheers. He tried to roll over, but the couch was too small and he ended up falling onto the floor, the wind knocked out of him and his face in the carpet.

"Oh, I'm sorry. Did I wake you?"

He opened his eyes a crack. A blurry image of Penny came into view. He scrambled to a sitting position. She was on her head, her elbows on the floor, toes pointed toward the ceiling. She wore a tight tank top and sweat pants.

"Why are you upside down?" Why did their conversations always turn into something bizarre?

She giggled. "Just doing my morning Yoga. There was more room in here. Sorry. I was trying to be quiet."

He stood and rubbed a hand over his stubbly face. "You're fine. I'll go take a shower." He shook his head and went into the bathroom. Taking *her* home to meet his stepmother was going to prove very interesting.

Penny stared out the car window and tried to swallow her nerves. All she had to do was go meet Harrison's family. It wasn't even anything formal. Show the stepmom proof that they were married, and get out of there. How hard could that be?

The flight to L.A. had been nice. She'd never flown first class before. The last flight she was on, she'd been stuffed between a grandmother and a burly man who wouldn't stop staring at her chest. This had been much roomier. And quieter.

Harrison had his driver, Antonio, pick them up. In his late fifties, Antonio was quite handsome, but his most notable feature was the intricate tattoo of an eagle that covered his neck and disappeared down under the collar of his shirt. Penny stared at it, curious about his background. How long had he worked for Harrison? She wondered what he got paid and if he just sat around all day waiting for a call to come drive Harrison somewhere. What a job.

The car pulled up to a large iron gate and the doors swung open. The largest house Penny had ever seen came into view. In fact, it didn't look like a house at all. It looked more like a spa resort. It was all columns and balconies and terraces, with beautiful landscaping. Her throat dried up and she sank down into her seat.

When the car stopped, Antonio hopped out and opened her door. For a split second she thought about cowering in the car and refusing to step into the sun, like some vampire who was about to get burned. She shook off the feeling. What could happen? She'd be fine.

She stepped onto the cobblestone drive, her high heels making her wobble. Antonio steadied her, and the eagle on his neck seemed to move. Fascinating. She wasn't used to wearing these shoes, but she figured she should look nice for Harrison's family. The skirt matched her heels, yellow with little white flowers. It flared out at the knees. Her tank top wasn't as nice as she wanted, but it would have to do.

Harrison slid out of the car and put his arm around her. His hand rested on her hip, sending shivers through her. Dang, he smelled good.

He smiled. "Are you ready?"

"No."

A warm laugh came out of him. "You'll be fine. She won't hurt you. Not in front of any witnesses."

Penny laughed, but then stopped when she realized she wasn't sure if he was joking or not. Harrison led her through an enormous door adorned with a Christmas wreath into a large foyer with marble flooring. It looked like a museum, with the grand chandelier, the art hanging on the walls, and the intricate detailing of the architecture. She hugged her middle, afraid to touch anything.

"So, you've returned."

Penny whipped around to see a younger version of Harrison standing a few feet away, wearing white tennis clothes. Harrison motioned to the man. "Penelope, this is my brother, Trent. Trent, Penelope Marie Ackerman."

She cringed at the use of her full name. Was that some rich person custom? How strange. "Hi." She held out her hand to shake his, but when he didn't move, she turned it into a wave.

Trent's gaze traveled the length of her, then he smiled. "You really know how to pick 'em, don't you?"

Stunned at his rude behavior, Penny's mouth fell open.

Harrison didn't seem to notice. "What's done is done. I've got a copy of the marriage license. I don't really care if Patrice doesn't like her."

Trent chuckled. "You might care when all hell rains down

on you. Did you have her sign a contract yet?" He motioned toward Penny.

Harrison shrugged and opened up his palms. "We just got here."

Penny elbowed Harrison in the ribs as hard as she could.

He let out a grunt, turning toward her. "What?"

"Really? You two are going to talk like I'm not standing *right here?*" She folded her arms across her chest.

Trent took a step toward her. "Forgive my rudeness, Penelope." He took her hand.

"It's Penny."

His smile widened. "Penny, then. I do apologize. I was just shocked when my brother announced he was married."

"Who's married?"

They turned to see two older women coming down the walkway. They both wore outfits that screamed, 'rich women with nothing better to do than dress up for afternoon tea.' One was decked out in pearls, while the other wore large red ruby earrings with matching lipstick.

Trent rocked back on his heels. "Harrison."

The color drained from Ruby Lips' face. "Excuse me?"

Dripping-With-Pearls clasped her hands together. "Patrice! Your son got married? I had no idea!"

Harrison cleared his throat and stepped forward. "Patrice, I'd like you to meet Penelope, my wife. Penelope, this is my stepmother, Patrice, and her good friend, Josephine."

Patrice's lips pressed into a thin line, her cheeks flushed, and for a second Penny thought she was going to explode. Then she smoothed out her features and smiled. "Why Harrison, this house must be too large. I didn't even know you were dating."

"It all happened kind of fast."

Josephine laughed, warm and loud. She grabbed Penny and patted her arm with her dainty white-gloved hands. "You must come with us. We were just getting ready for tea. I want to hear all about this whirlwind courtship."

Penny held in a giggle. How had she guessed it was tea time? "That sounds delightful."

"Come, boys, you will join us for tea." Patrice left no room for argument.

"What Patrice commands…" Harrison muttered under his breath.

Patrice shot him a glare that could melt glass. After they were seated—and were served by a girl they'd probably hired just to serve tea—Josephine turned to Harrison. "Tell us, how did you two meet?"

He squirmed a bit before answering. "We met in Las Vegas. The city of love."

Trent frowned. "Isn't that Paris?" He jumped, like he'd been kicked under the table.

"It was the city of love for us, right, Penelope?"

She resisted the urge to shout, "It's Penny!" and slap him upside the head. Instead, she nodded. "Yes. It was instant love."

Patrice narrowed her eyes and sipped her tea. "Didn't you fly into Las Vegas yesterday?"

Harrison nodded. "Right after the plane landed, I met Penelope. We spent an amazing day together, and that's when I realized I didn't want to spend another one without her. We got married on the spot. I have a copy of the marriage license—"

"Congratulations, Bro." Trent clapped him on the back.

Patrice bristled, then shifted in her chair. "Well, I must say, this is all very shocking, indeed."

"Oh, I think it's romantic." Josephine waved away Patrice's concern. "This will be a great story to tell their grandkids someday." It was obvious Josephine was enjoying this situation immensely. Maybe because she'd just learned the juiciest gossip of the week and couldn't wait to blab it all over the neighborhood.

Harrison covered Penny's hand with his own. "Yes, romantic. That's what we were going for."

Patrice didn't look convinced, so Penny looped her arm around Harrison's. "This really has been a crazy twenty-four hours. But I can't imagine spending the rest of my life with anyone else."

Patrice raised her eyebrow in a classic 'Oh, really?' gesture, which irked Penny. Who was she to imply they weren't in love? To prove it, she leaned over and kissed Harrison full on the lips.

The kiss must have surprised him, because he started to jerk his head back, which totally would have given them away.

So Penny wrapped her arms around his neck and hung on like a suckerfish.

At first, he just sat there, unmoving. It was like kissing a statue. Well, a statue that smelled amazing. But then he probably realized he needed to do something or she'd never let go. He pulled her close and moved his lips against hers.

The kiss started out lukewarm but quickly turned fire engine hot. Tingling sensations zipped through her and she grew light headed. His lips were warm and soft, but sent lightning through her wherever they touched. It was both thrilling and enticing. When she finally ended the kiss, both women were staring at them with wide eyes.

Trent was trying not to laugh.

Josephine fanned her face. "Well, I say, they most certainly look like they're in love."

Patrice didn't say anything, but sat with pinched lips.

Harrison stared at Penny, like he was seeing her for the first time. Then he stood. "Thank you for tea, Mother. It was a delight, as always. We must go unpack."

Patrice stood as well. "A pleasure to meet you, dear." She grabbed Penny's hand, her talon-like fingernails digging into her skin. "You will be joining us for supper, won't you?"

Penny tried to jerk her hand away, but the woman had it in a vice-grip. "Yes," she said, hoping the old bat would let go if she agreed to eat with her.

"Good. We shall see you at six o'clock then." The woman gave her one more squeeze, digging her nails in deeper, pulling Penny closer. Before releasing her, she hissed in her ear, "You'll regret this."

CHAPTER 5

Penny swallowed a yelp and pulled away from the crazy woman. No one else had noticed. Her hand throbbed, but she didn't want to make a scene, so she put it behind her back. Harrison turned to leave, and Penny followed close behind. When they were out of earshot she nudged him, holding out her hand.

"Look what your stepmother did to me." The fingernail marks were an angry purple against her skin.

Harrison grabbed her hand to examine it. "She did this?"

Penny nodded.

"She's gone too far this time." He clenched his jaw and turned toward her.

Penny grabbed his arm. "Wait. Don't."

"I can't let her get away with this." The anger and concern on his face on her behalf touched her.

She smiled. "Oh, I have no intention of letting her get away with it. But now isn't the time." She patted his hand. "I'll deal with her later."

His eyes narrowed. "What are you going to do?"

She had no idea, but the old witch had declared war. "Something I'll probably regret."

To her surprise, Harrison let out a laugh. He put his arm around her shoulders. "Life is never boring around you, is it?"

He led her past a huge Christmas tree decorated with gold ribbon and white lights. They went up the stairs, down a hall past several doors, and into a bedroom. Dark wood tones were accented with deep reds, which gave it a masculine feel. A king sized bed took up half the room, and a cozy recliner sat by a glass door leading to a balcony. The house must have been built on a cliff, because the view overlooking L.A. was amazing. She opened a door and found a huge walk-in closet. She stared at the shelves and racks of clothes. His closet was larger than her childhood bedroom.

"You can take the left side."

Penny didn't realize Harrison had followed her in, and she whipped around, running into his chest. A rock-solid chest. Oh, boy. She took a step back to try to clear her head. "Okay."

His lips twitched like he was trying not to smile. "You're cute when you're flustered."

She stared at him. What was he doing, flirting with her? Maybe that kiss had given him courage or something. It had been pretty hot. But didn't he realize that she and William—her thoughts stopped abruptly. There was no 'she and William' anymore. The reality of it hit her and tears sprang to her eyes.

Harrison's eyebrows pushed together and he lifted her chin. "Hey, I was only kidding. I didn't mean anything by it."

"I know." She blinked the tears away. "I'm just missing William."

He opened his mouth like he wanted to say something,

but stopped himself. Instead, he pulled her close, wrapping his strong arms around her. "I'm sorry."

Her heart thundered in her chest as she breathed in his cologne. Conflicting feelings overwhelmed her and she backed out of his embrace. "Don't be. I'll get over it."

She left the closet and wandered over to the spacious bathroom. There was a shower, a tub, three sinks and two full-length mirrors. Man, she could probably fit her entire graduating class in here. Granted, she grew up in a small town, but really, who needs a bathroom that can fit fifty people? "Nice Jacuzzi."

Harrison nodded but didn't say anything. What was he thinking? Probably that she was a nutcase. She sure felt like one.

"So, um." Harrison rubbed the back of his neck. "You can have the bed. I'll sleep in the chair."

That's what he was thinking about. Sleeping arrangements. Nice of him to give up the bed again. Chivalrous. Like something William would do. Another twinge of pain rippled through her. "Thanks."

She needed to stop thinking about him, that's what she needed to do. She grasped at anything to get her mind off William. "How many bedrooms does this place have?"

"Twelve."

"Wow. Who all lives here?"

Harrison walked over to the sliding glass door. "Just my stepmother and me. Trent lives over in Beverly Hills with his wife."

Seemed pretty wasteful to have such a large house with hardly anyone in it. But that would have been rude to say. "What about your servants?"

He chuckled. "Servants? You mean the staff?"

Oops. She had called them the wrong thing. Heat flushed her cheeks, but she ignored it and nodded.

"Antonio lives in an apartment above the garage. The rest of the staff have their own homes." His eyes twinkled with a hidden smile.

"You grew up here?" She sat down on the bed and slipped off her heels.

"Yes."

There was a sadness to his voice, but she didn't want to pry. "How come you've never moved out?"

He lifted one shoulder. "I always planned to, after I got my trust fund."

"But you have to be married to get that." She cocked her head to the side. He was handsome, and rich. Surely he didn't have to resort to marrying a stranger. "Why are you doing all this, anyway? Wouldn't it have been easier to find a real wife?"

He sighed and shoved his fists in his pockets, turning to look out at the view. "I did." He clenched his jaw. "It didn't work out."

Seeing him in obvious turmoil made her heart ache. "Divorced?"

"No. Thankfully, I found out what kind of woman she was before the wedding."

"Well, that's good."

He turned to her, a pained expression on his face. "An hour before, actually."

"Oh. Not good." The poor guy. She felt bad for him but was too curious not to ask. "You find her with another man?"

He cringed. "The best man."

"That's horrible. What did you do?" She ran her hand over the soft coverlet on his bed.

He frowned. "She begged me not to tell anyone. Said it would ruin her socially. She pleaded with me, and I felt bad for her. So I walked away. Everyone thought I left her at the altar."

"What? *You* got blamed for it?" Indignation arose in her.

"Yes. The wedding was kind of a big deal. Lots of publicity. Leaving her at the altar was not looked upon very favorably. Let's just say I haven't been on many dates since then."

"I can't believe she did that to you."

He shrugged. "She cared more about her reputation than mine."

Penny tried to imagine what it would be like to have everyone think you did something horrible when in fact, you were the one hurting. It wasn't a pleasant thought, and she stared down at her hands. How awful it must have been for him. She could tell by his body language—back straight, his fists clenched—that he was still bothered by it, even though he tried to act nonchalant.

She hopped off the bed. "Come on, let's do something fun before dinner. You guys have a pool, right?"

He raised an eyebrow. "Yes."

"Let's go swimming. It's totally warm outside."

A frown pulled down the corners of his mouth and he folded his arms across his chest. "I'm not really the swimming pool type."

He didn't use his pool? For some reason that bothered her more than the unused bedrooms. "Well, you're going to be today. Get your swim trunks on."

She didn't wait to see if he obeyed. She walked into the closet and shut the door, then dug through her suitcase until she found her faded suit. It had seen better days, but it still fit so it was difficult to justify buying a new one. She slipped it on and called out to Harrison. "You decent?"

"Yes."

She opened the closet and peered out. Harrison stood facing the sliding glass door, his casual clothes still on. She huffed. "Why aren't you in your swim trunks?"

"I thought you were kidding." He turned and his gaze froze on her.

"No, I wasn't. Get your suit on!"

He sighed, but walked to his dresser and opened a drawer. "All right."

She waited while he went into the bathroom to change. Her phone sat on top of the dresser, and she picked it up. There were a few messages from William that she'd missed. He was pleading with her to forgive him. Tears threatened to spill down her cheeks, but she blinked them away.

She slid open the balcony door and stepped out, clutching her phone. Two patio chairs faced the amazing view, overlooking LA. A light breeze carried a woodsy scent mixed with a lighter floral smell.

A noise sounded below and she peered down to see Patrice on a stone walkway. The rail thin woman glanced around as if she was nervous someone was following her. Then she continued toward the garage.

What was up with that? Penny assumed Patrice could go anywhere she wanted. Why was she acting all sneaky like? Whatever.

Penny sighed and plopped down in one of the chairs. William lived in Santa Barbara. Just an hour and a half away. She stared down at the phone in her hand.

"Nice view, huh?"

Harrison's voice startled her, and she jumped, then felt guilty for being caught thinking about William. "Yeah."

He sat down on the other chair, and she choked back a gasp. Who knew under that suit he was so ripped? He wasn't body builder material or anything, but his well-defined muscles made her heart pound in her chest. Holy cow, she needed to get out more.

"I like to sit out here in the evenings." He steepled his fingers and tapped his chin. "It's peaceful."

She tore her gaze away from his chest. "I can see that."

They sat for a minute in comfortable silence. Then Harrison shifted in his seat. "You still going to drag me down to the pool?"

"You betcha." She hopped up and grabbed his hand. Electricity zinged through her, and she dropped it. "Come on. Last one in is a loser."

He stood, his eyes hiding a smile. "You don't even know the way."

"How hard can it be? I'll bet I can be in the pool even before you've left your room."

He arched a brow. "Sounds like a challenge."

They stared at each other for a second before they both took off, running through Harrison's bedroom and down the hallway. Penny's bare feet slapped against the marble tile as she tried to get in front of him. She was faster on the stairs and ended up being several feet ahead. Not knowing quite where to go, but following her instinct, she took off toward the west end of the house.

She ran through several rooms—a sitting room, one with a piano, a formal dining room—but when she rounded a corner she collided with a woman carrying a tray of dirty dishes. Teacups and saucers clattered to the floor and the woman shouted something in Spanish.

"Oh! I'm sorry!" Penny turned and Harrison ran smack into her, knocking her on her behind. Harrison's face almost made her laugh out loud, his eyes were so wide.

The Spanish woman set the tray on the counter and began picking up dishes. "Lo siento, señor Williams!"

Penny scrambled to help her. "It's my fault. I shouldn't have been running." She picked up a broken teacup. "I hope this wasn't valuable."

"The set has only been in the family for a hundred years." The cold voice was unmistakable, and Penny cringed. She looked up to see Patrice staring down at her, contempt darkening her eyes.

Heat rushed to Penny's cheeks and she rose. "I'm sorry—"

"Save your apologies for the stupid. I'm not blind. I know what's going on here."

"Patrice!" Harrison stepped between them, shielding Penny from his stepmother. "You can't treat my wife this way."

"Your *wife?*" She spat the word out like a spoiled piece of meat. "You mean this hussy? She's simply a mistake that will soon be rectified. And you will not disrespect me. I am your *mother.*" She pointed a long red fingernail in his face. "I may not have birthed you, but I raised you."

"You mean you paid the nannies who raised me," he said under his breath.

"Don't sass me. I won't stand to be mocked in my own house." She turned and left the room, and Penny swore she heard a crack of thunder as the woman departed.

Harrison turned to Penny. "I'm sorry about that. I didn't think she would react this way—by attacking you. Are you okay?"

She was too stunned to speak, so she just nodded.

"She's been bothering me to get married for years. One would think she'd be happy about it." His frown deepened. "Come on. I'll show you the way to the pool."

"I wasn't headed there?"

His laugh lines crinkled with his smile. "Not even close."

CHAPTER 6

Harrison sat on the side of the pool, dangling his legs in the water. It had been years since he'd been swimming. It was surprisingly relaxing. He and Penny had swum a few laps, then she'd gotten out of the pool to pump up a floating lounge chair. He watched her get in the water and struggle to get on it. She'd get one leg on, and then the whole thing would float out of her grasp. He chuckled, then realized he was staring at her legs. She had curves in all the right places.

The third time she fell off the lounge he jumped in the water and swam over to her. "Here, let me hold it. That'll be easier."

"Thanks." After she was on, she grinned like a little kid. "This is fun. You should get on."

"That's a one-person chair."

She giggled, and something stirred in him.

He liked her. He couldn't deny it. When she'd kissed him, he'd been surprised to find himself attracted to her. More than that. Something had awakened in him that had been dead for a long time. He hadn't wanted to stop kissing her.

And now he needed to tear his gaze away from her lips. She was speaking. What was she saying?

"You'd fit. It's a huge floaty."

He laughed. "I'll make it tip over." Even though it was ridiculous, he suddenly wanted to climb up there with her. He'd have to snuggle pretty close to keep it from capsizing. The thought made him smile.

"No, you won't." She scooted over then patted the seat. "Come on, I dare you."

He grabbed the sides and heaved his upper body up, which bounced Penny and she squealed. "Hang on," he said while getting another hold on the sides. In order to keep the chair afloat, he basically had to climb on top of her.

She giggled again when he maneuvered to lay beside her. The chair rocked dangerously, but didn't tip over. "You did it." She smiled up at him.

He propped his head up on his hand and stared at her lips. What would she do if he kissed her?

Her eyes met his, and she blushed under the intensity of his gaze. "What are you thinking about?" Her voice was so quiet, he could barely hear her.

His desire to kiss her overwhelmed him. How would she react? The kiss they'd shared at tea had been amazing. Would every kiss with her be like that? There was only one way to find out.

He half-shrugged. "About you." He moved closer. "About this." He brushed his lips across hers, and she closed her eyes. He took that as a good sign and deepened the kiss. Sensations washed over him as he let instinct take the lead. Penny pressed her hand against his chest, her touch sending heat through him. Kissing her was like nothing he'd ever experienced before. Sure, there'd been passion with Carol, but had been a tiny flame compared to this raging fire.

Penny's pulse raced as Harrison kissed her. Dang, he knew how to kiss. She had to use all her will power not to wrap her arms around him. She couldn't. She wasn't over William yet. It was stupid to love William, she knew that. But she couldn't help it. He'd been her best friend for two years. Kissing Harrison was wrong. And she was going to stop. Any minute now.

Her phone called out "Text Message" by the side of the pool and she jerked her head back, scrambling away from Harrison. Unfortunately, the movement caused the chair to rock, sending her over the side with a yelp. Cold water doused the flames that Harrison had ignited and startled her out of the haze she'd been in.

William was texting.

She surfaced and realized the chair had capsized with Harrison in it.

He swam over to her, smiling, and pulled her to him.

But she wriggled out of his grasp. "I'm sorry. That was a mistake. I can't."

Her phone sounded again. "Text Message!"

His smile disappeared and he cocked his head to the side, scrutinizing her. When her phone sounded a third time, he motioned toward it. "Go. Answer him."

She swam away from him, a strange sense of loss tugging at her heart. She climbed out of the pool and dried off. Her legs wobbled as she picked up her phone and swiped to read the message.

W: Your silent treatment is killing me.

W: Please say something. I'm sorry. U are the most important person in the world to me. I never meant to hurt u.

W: I want to work this out. U mean so much to me. Please text me back. I love u.

His pleadings stabbed at her heart. She couldn't stand to ignore him any longer, even though she still hurt from what he'd done.

P: I thought you loved me.

W: I do, Penny! Please forgive me. I don't know what I was thinking.

P: I thought you wanted to get married.

W: I'm so sorry. I have to be honest. I don't think I'm ready.

The words stung Penny. He'd lied about being held up. She'd known he had, but this proved it.

W: Don't think poorly of me, sweetheart. It is hard for me to admit, but I think I have commitment issues.

That might explain a few things. She punched in her response.

P: You have issues, all right.

W: I do. I'm sorry. I think we should meet. Just to talk.

The thought of meeting William made her pulse race. After all this time, meeting him face to face was something she felt she needed. She tried to push out of her mind the reality that she'd expected to meet him yesterday—at the altar.

She hesitated, not sure of what she should say to him. She wanted to meet. She loved him. Working things out just made sense, right? She typed her response.

P: Yes. We should meet.

Harrison pulled himself out of the pool and started toward her. She quickly typed the rest.

P: I have to go now. I will text u later.

She switched her phone off and turned to Harrison. Water glistened on his muscled chest, causing her breath to catch and she forced herself to avert her eyes. "Thanks for swimming with me. I think I'll go back up and change now."

His gaze probed hers. "Sure. I'll take you up." He grabbed a towel and rubbed his head and chest.

She followed him through the house and up to the bedroom. The door was ajar, and when she entered she saw why. A note lay on the bed. She picked it up.

You will dress up for dinner tonight. I have friends coming over and you will not embarrass me.

Patrice

Harrison spoke from behind her. "What's that?"

She turned, letting out a frustrated breath. "Your wicked stepmother wants to make sure I don't embarrass her tonight." Penny flicked the note onto the bed.

"Appearances mean more to her than anything. Don't take it personally." He reached out to her like he was going to touch her, but then withdrew his hand as if he'd thought better of it. "She doesn't even know you."

"Yeah, well, she definitely doesn't like me."

He closed his eyes and ran his hand through his dark hair. "It's my fault. I embarrassed her in front of her socialite friend. It's me she's mad at. I just didn't think—"

"It's okay. I can take care of myself. But she'd better watch out."

He smiled. "She's more upset than I thought. You might want to stay away from her wrath. Fly below the radar until I can get the trust fund and get you out of here."

Penny raised her chin. "Just remember—she attacked first."

CHAPTER 7

Harrison adjusted his tie in the bathroom mirror, staring at his reflection. What was he doing, trying to impress Penny? He let out a breath. She didn't seem to be the type to care what he was wearing. In fact, she'd let him know how stupid she thought it was to dress up for dinner. She hadn't intended on changing, but he'd convinced her it was a good idea. She'd rummaged through her suitcase and found a sundress, which she looked amazing in. He'd had to get out of the bedroom because he couldn't stop staring at her legs.

When it was time to go down to dinner, he walked over to her and offered her his elbow. She was curled up on his chair, surfing the web on his laptop. She took his arm, her touch sending warmth through him. He smiled down at her, hoping she felt the same growing attraction he was feeling. She blushed and lowered her lashes. Maybe there could be something between them.

Penny was impulsive, but she was also warm and more down to earth than any other woman he'd dated. She made him feel like she really cared, whereas the rest of them dated him for his money and social status. Thinking about having a relationship with Penny made him excited. Happy even.

"Wait." Penny withdrew her hand. "I'd better tell William I'm going to be away for a while." She ran over to the nightstand and picked up her phone.

Harrison exhaled. What was he thinking? She was still hung up on this Internet guy she'd never even met. He swallowed his disappointment. They were silent as he walked her down to the sitting room.

Patrice stood when they entered. Her gaze traveled over Penny and a disapproving frown settled on her face. "Didn't you get my note?"

Penny's eyes widened, and Harrison steeled himself. "Mother. Stop."

Patrice plastered on a fake smile. "I want you to meet my closest friends. This is Eleanor Watkins and Miranda Henning. And of course you met Josephine Gilbert earlier today." Patrice reached out to take Penny's hand, but judging from what happened earlier Harrison didn't think that was a good idea, so he stepped in between them. Unfortunately, that pushed Penny a little and she stumbled. Harrison steadied her, before she ended up on the floor.

Patrice glared at him, but quickly recovered. "Your brother will be here soon, and then we'll go into the other room."

Harrison sat on the loveseat with Penny. Eleanor, a skinny old woman with a long horse-like face, leaned toward them. "I hear you two had a whirlwind wedding." Her smile was all teeth. "Do tell me about it."

"Oh, yes, it was crazy all right," Penny said, grabbing his hand. "We fell in love and threw caution to the wind!"

Miranda, who was more round than tall, spoke up. "Did you really marry the day you met?" She raised an eyebrow, as if she didn't believe it.

"Yes," Harrison said.

The old ladies all gasped, and Patrice looked like she wanted to sink into the carpet. She picked up a champagne glass and took a sip.

Penny giggled. "It was quite romantic. I mean, I didn't even know Harrison was worth billions."

Patrice choked on her drink, and Harrison could feel the blood drain from his face. Penny continued. "But, luckily for him, I don't care about his money. I'm just a small town girl from Iowa. What would I do with a million dollars?"

Harrison stared at her.

The women's jaws were just about on the floor.

Miranda composed herself first. "You mean, you married him before you knew who he was?"

"Well, I knew I was in love. That's all that matters, right?" Penny's wide eyes gave her the look of an innocent doe. Either that or a serial killer who was out of touch with reality.

Miranda must have been thinking serial killer, because she scooted back in her chair.

Josephine laughed and tugged on her white gloves. "You are a delight, girl. You must come to the Christmas soirée I'm having this weekend. Everyone who is anyone will be there."

Patrice, Miranda, and Eleanor looked at Josephine like she'd suggested they all dance on the table naked.

A look of apprehension crossed Penny's face, but she smoothed it out. "I'd love to."

Trent entered the room with his wife. Last summer when Harrison first met her, he'd had to blink to make sure she was real. She had platinum-blonde hair, an unnaturally thin waist, a perfectly perky chest, and legs so long he wondered how she kept from falling over. It was like she'd handed her plastic surgeon a Barbie doll for reference and he'd taken her seriously. Her name was Candy. Of course.

After Trent introduced Candy to Penny, they all went into the formal dining room. It was more like a hall than a room, with a table so long it would seat twenty. Harrison couldn't remember a time when they'd filled it. Penny must think they were insane. He was beginning to agree.

Annabel brought out the hors d'oeuvres—escargot in garlic butter, served with artichoke hearts and caviar. Penny picked up her tongs and raised an eyebrow. "What are these things? They look like eyelash curlers or something."

Candy giggled. "Those are tongs. You hold the shells with them. Then you dig out the inside with the fork."

Penny's face brightened. "Like in Pretty Woman when Julia Roberts flung the snail guts across the room."

Harrison hid a smile. Patrice scoffed and straightened in her chair, surely too proper to admit to having seen a movie like Pretty Woman. Eleanor peered at Penny over her glasses.

Josephine laughed. "Slippery little suckers. What a great line. I love that movie."

"I'll try not to sail my appetizer across the room." Penny picked up her fork and started digging in the shell. She pulled the escargot out and put it in her mouth, then looked around the room, probably noticing that everyone was watching her. "Mmm," she said.

Josephine clapped, which didn't really work with her white gloves on. "Bravo!"

Patrice held a tight smile. "Penelope, do tell us. What exactly is it that you do?"

"I'm a performer. I sing, and dance."

A smug look crossed Patrice's face. "Ah, I see. I suppose there are poles involved in your dance routine?"

Heat rose to Harrison's face, and he clenched his fists. "Patrice!" Harrison didn't disguise the anger in his voice. She was going too far.

Penny waved it away. "Oh, no, not that kind of dancing.

More like what you'd see on Broadway. Why, Patrice, you probably know what I'm talking about, having grown up in that area."

Everyone turned to look at Patrice. The color drained from her face. "I beg your pardon. I'm from California."

"Oh, I'm sorry. I could have sworn I heard you were from Queens." The smile on Penny's face widened. "What was it your father did again? I thought he was—"

"I've never been to Iowa," Patrice interrupted. "Tell me about it."

Harrison stared at his stepmother as Penny went into a monologue about Iowa and growing up in a small town surrounded by corn fields. Patrice grew up in Queens? Oh, that was too good. Harrison could hardly believe it. She'd put on airs and told everyone her father was some rich son of a gold miner. He wondered what the truth was.

The rest of the meal went without incident. They ate some fancy sushi junk his stepmother loved. He realized he'd rather be eating at Lord of the Onion Rings. As he walked Penny back to their room, he whispered, "How did you find out about Queens?"

"It's amazing what you can find on the Internet if you have a valid credit card number."

He raised an eyebrow. "You have a valid credit card number?"

She looked up at him, a smile in her eyes. "No. But you do."

Before they made it to their door, Patrice stepped out from around a corner, stopping them. She pointed a finger at Penny. "I don't know how you found out, you little viper, but I will not tolerate blackmail." She turned to Harrison. "As for you, I spoke with my attorney this afternoon. I have changed the conditions. You now have to be married for two years before you get the trust."

Penny's eyes widened and Harrison's mouth went dry. "What? You can't do that," he said.

A satisfied smirk settled on her face. "I can, and I did. This is not a game, but if it were, I would win. I always do." She took a step back. "I won't be played for a fool."

Penny muttered, "Well, if it walks like a duck…"

His stepmother's face turned a deep shade of purple, and she looked like she wanted to choke the life out of Penny. "You will not get a dime of this family's money." She rounded the corner, the clicking of her shoes on the tile fading down the hall.

CHAPTER 8

Penny pushed Harrison into the bedroom and shut the door, trying not to panic. "Two years? We can't stay married for two years." She kept her voice low, even though she wanted to shout. Her throat closed and she struggled to breathe. This wasn't happening. Not now. Not when William was making strides and seemed ready to commit. Or at least work on things.

Harrison paced the room, his distress evident in the way he scrubbed his hand over his face. "I know, I know. We'll contest it. I'll figure something out."

"You'd better," she said, stabbing the air with her finger. "William apologized. He wants to meet. I think he—" She stopped talking when she saw the look on Harrison's face. "What?"

Harrison swallowed, and took a step toward her. "William wants to meet you?" He worked his jaw muscles. "Do you think that's…wise?"

"I know William better than anyone. He would never hurt me."

"Like he would never leave you at the altar." He advanced.

Her heart sped up as he drew closer. "He's not perfect. He made a mistake." The smell of Harrison's cologne was messing with her head. Made it hard to think. She sank down on the bed. "He didn't mean to hurt me."

Harrison sighed and sat down beside her. He looked like he wanted to lecture her, but instead he simply said, "How did you two meet?"

She shrugged, since it wasn't any big deal. "We met in a chat room." When he didn't respond, she elaborated. "Don't Blink."

He raised an eyebrow, and she giggled. He looked adorable with that puzzled expression. "Don't Blink is a chat room for Whovians."

"Speak English, please."

She laughed. "Your lack of nerd knowledge is cute. We just met online. That's all that's important."

"So, what, his profile pic was hot, so you started chatting with him?"

"His profile pic was a TARDIS."

Harrison blinked, obviously lost. "What's that?"

"That blue police box The Doctor uses." When his blank look got even blanker, she smiled. "Forget it. It's a *Doctor Who* thing."

"Oh. How did you end up in Las Vegas, standing at an altar?"

Penny slipped off her shoes and scooted back on the bed. "William kept bugging me to go away for a weekend with him. I told him I wasn't going to do that until I was married. Then he said, 'Well, why don't we?' and I said, 'Do what?' and he said, 'Get married. You live in Las Vegas.' And then I said, 'Are you serious?!?' and he said, 'Yes.'" She picked a piece of lint off her dress, too embarrassed to look up at Harrison. "I guess he wasn't as serious as I was."

Harrison was silent for a moment. Then he quietly said,

"So he wanted a weekend of fun, and you wanted a lifetime commitment."

She glared at him. "Well, when you put it that way, it sounds like I was trying to push him into something. But he's the one who suggested it."

"Only to get what he wanted from you."

Heat rose to her face, and she hopped off the bed. "You're a pig!"

He stood as well. "*Men* are pigs, Penny. It's not safe for you to go off to meet some guy from the Internet. Do you even know what he looks like?"

She grabbed her phone. "Yes. He sent me a photo." After flipping through her images, she shoved it in his face.

He squinted. "Is he the blurry one, or the bald guy in back?"

She scoffed. "The blurry one, of course."

"Good. Because the other dude has some serious Danny Devito thing going on. I think you'd tower over him."

"Funny. But like I said, that's not him. William is tall and handsome, as you can see."

The look on Harrison's face was difficult to interpret. He handed the phone back. "If you insist on going to meet him, at least take me along. For safety reasons."

The thought had occurred to her. She didn't really want to drive by herself in an unfamiliar place. Especially on the scary freeways of California. "Fine."

"Fine." He folded his arms across his chest. "When are we going?"

"I'll ask William."

She could have sworn she saw him roll his eyes, but he turned away from her too quickly to tell. "Fine," he muttered.

She gripped her phone and went into the closet to change. Five minutes later she was stretched out on the deck in her yoga pants, texting William.

W: Tomorrow? Um, I don't think tomorrow is good for me.

P: When, then?

W: Next weekend. I'll take u to dinner.

P: Great. But, um, can I bring a friend?

W: A friend? On our first date?

P: That does sound like a bad idea. It's just—I promised I'd bring him along.

W: Him? You want to bring a guy with u? What's going on, Penny?

P: He thinks it's a bad idea for me to meet u.

W: Who is this guy??

P: My husband.

W: What??? You said you were single!

P: I am!! I mean, I was. Until u didn't show up. The limo driver picked up the wrong guy at the airport.

W: You're serious? You married a stranger?

P: I thought he was you!!

W: I'm getting a headache.

P: What restaurant should we meet at?

W: I changed my mind. We shouldn't meet.

P: Don't be like that.

W: But u want to bring your husband on a date with me. You don't see anything wrong with that?

P: I don't love him like I love you.

"What does he say?" The deep sound of Harrison's voice startled Penny and she jumped, hugging her phone to her chest.

"Don't do that!"

He sat down on the other lounge chair, his laptop in his hand. He'd changed into a T-shirt and shorts. "Do what?"

"Sneak up on me. It's not nice." She shot him a glare.

"Well, what's he saying?"

Her phone screeched "Text message," and she pushed the button.

W: I love u 2. But you need to get this situation resolved before we meet.

Penny frowned. "He doesn't want to meet now that I've told him you're coming along."

He raised an eyebrow. "See? He doesn't have good intentions. Do you even know his last name?"

Anger and frustration boiled in her. "Yes. It's Tucker. And he just doesn't want me to bring my husband on our date! Don't you see anything wrong with that?"

The corner of his mouth quirked in a smile. "Well, when you put it like that."

She wanted to throw something at him, but nothing was around, so she grunted and folded her arms across her chest. "You're impossible."

He reached over and touched her arm, and she tried to ignore the tingles it caused. "I'm only trying to keep you safe."

She knew it was true. Harrison did want to keep her safe. Unfortunately, he was messing everything up with William. She huffed and hopped off her chair. "Good night." She stormed into the other room and slipped under the covers.

~

Harrison stared at his laptop screen, the window Penny had opened tempting him like siren call. Privateeyes4u.com boasted amazing results in less than an hour. Police records, background checks, birth records—you could get it all for under a hundred dollars.

Penny wouldn't have to know, right? He could dig up some information on William, just to make sure the guy wasn't a serial rapist or anything. It was for her own good. In fact, if she were thinking straight, she'd want him to do it.

He typed William's name and cell phone number into the form and clicked. After putting in his credit card information and getting a receipt, he closed his laptop and took a deep breath.

He'd done the right thing. Penny needed to be protected.

So why did he feel so guilty?

CHAPTER 9

*P*enny sat up in bed, unsure of what had awakened her. Must have been a noise of some sort. Maybe Harrison was snoring. She peered over into the darkness. The recliner sat empty, the blanket he had been using draped across the arm. The bathroom door was open, the light off. Where was he? She looked at the clock. One-thirty.

Her stomach growled, and she slid out of bed. Harrison had probably gone down to the kitchen to get something to eat, which sounded like a good idea to her. She grabbed her phone and used it as a flashlight, sneaking through the house until she saw the kitchen light shining under the door.

She figured she'd see Harrison in there. What she didn't expect was to find him at the counter, apron on, furiously chopping onions on a cutting board.

"What are you—"

He turned with a start, knife pointed at her, eyes wide.

"Whoa. Put that thing down."

"Sorry, you startled me." He lowered the knife. "I thought you were Patrice."

"I can see why you'd want a knife in that case."

His deep laugh filled the room, making her smile. He turned back to his chopping. "What are you doing up?"

She crossed the room to stand beside him. "Woke up hungry. That raw fish stuff was fine, but not very filling."

He made a face. "Yeah."

Several small glass bowls sat in front of him, various chopped items in them. A skillet and a carton of eggs sat on the stove. "Omelets?"

He grinned. "I watched Chef Ramsey make an omelet on Food Network the other day. I've been craving them ever since."

Penny's mouth dropped. "You watch Food Network?"

He lifted one shoulder. "Sometimes."

She stared at him. "You're a foodie."

"A what? No I'm not." He pulled a package of pepperoni out of the fridge.

"Yes, you are. Just look at you, all dolled up in an apron, chopping up all kinds of crazy things to put in your omelet. You're grinning like a twelve year old whose fart got blamed on his sister."

He laughed, the warm, richness of it washing over her. "You're insane."

"Deny it all you want. You, my dear, are a foodie."

He shook his head and continued to chop the remaining slices of pepperoni. "You want one?"

"Sure."

He cracked eggs into a separator and began whipping the whites. As he worked, she studied him. He seemed so much more relaxed, like he was in his element. He carried a hint of a smile, and he handled the spatula in a natural way, like he'd been doing it forever. If he opened up a restaurant he'd have a blast with it. She slid onto a stool at the built-in bar.

He pulled two plates from the cupboard and flipped an omelet onto one and handed it to her. She picked up her fork and cut into it. The eggs were fluffy and melted in her mouth. "This is delicious."

His smile widened, but he didn't say anything. The silence was comfortable, though, and when he was done making his omelet he sat beside her and ate.

"What made you think to put pepperoni in here? It adds the perfect zing to it."

He shrugged. "Just thought it would be good."

"Well, it is. You have great instinct." A blush crept up his neck and Penny held in a laugh.

"I actually wanted to go to culinary school instead of business school."

"Really?" Penny was stunned. "You'd be an awesome chef. Why didn't you?"

"Because," said a cold voice behind them.

Penny whipped around to see Patrice standing there, her arms folded across her chest.

"No son of mine is going to become a *cook*." She spat the word, like it tasted bitter on her tongue.

Harrison sighed and turned to face her. "Hello, Mother."

Blood colored Patrice's cheeks, and she glared at them. "Clean up this mess when you're done. I don't want the staff spreading rumors about you."

Penny sprang from her stool, unable to hold it in any longer. "Rumors? Because he got hungry and made an omelet?"

Patrice took two steps back, her nightgown flowing around her ankles. "Penelope—"

"It's Penny!" It came out a little more forceful than she'd meant, but it did the job. Patrice blinked and then started again.

"Penny, I'm sure you grew up in a very different environment, so these things would be difficult to understand."

"Oh, I understand just fine. You've mistakenly equated money and status with happiness."

Patrice clicked her tongue and frowned. "It's so simple to you, isn't it?" Her tone dripped of condescension. "Life doesn't work that way. You see, Harrison must keep up certain appearances in order for people to have confidence in Harrison Williams Investment Group. Without investments, the company goes under, and we go under along with it." She looked down her nose. "You might imagine our money sitting in a bank, easy to access, just waiting for us to spend it. You'd be wrong. We are worth billions because of Harrison Williams Investment Group. Without the business, we have nothing."

"Don't be so dramatic," Harrison said.

"And don't you let this floozy fill your head with nonsense. You know your duty."

"Stop! That's enough. I will not allow you to insult her. It was just a question. She didn't mean anything by it."

Patrice smiled, which looked rather scary on her. "Of course." She stared at Penny for a moment before she turned and padded out of the kitchen. "Have a good night."

When Penny was sure she was gone, she sank back onto her stool. "Man, she is awful. How do you stand it?"

Harrison broke out into a grin. "I just imagine her head as a giant hot air balloon."

A laugh bubbled up. "She looked like a ripe tomato tonight." Penny blew out her cheeks and held her breath.

"You do a great impression of her."

Penny blew out her breath and turned serious. She ran the tips of her fingers along the edge of the counter. "Is the company in trouble?"

Harrison shook his head. "No."

"Then why is she so uptight about it?"

"I don't think she's really worried about the business. She

thinks the culinary arts are beneath me." He picked up their empty plates and took them to the sink.

Penny hopped off her stool and picked up the little glass bowls, setting them in the sink as well. "I don't understand. There are many famous chefs out there making a decent living."

"Cooking for other people. It's a service profession." He turned on the faucet and pushed the stopper in.

"So is making investments for people, right? You have customers. You have to make them happy."

He frowned. "She doesn't see it that way."

As they finished the dishes, Penny grew sad for him. He was stuck in a job he didn't like, building a business he didn't care about, all for money that wasn't making him happy. If only he could see how this was sucking the life out of him.

They went upstairs in silence.

⁓

Penny knew it was a dream. Her head floated in that funny cloudy way, and her legs wouldn't work right. She was trying to climb the stairs to get to William. Who knew why she thought William would be at the top of the stairs. Dreams didn't make sense. But for some reason she urgently needed to get to him.

And then Harrison was there, his handsome face before her. He put his hands on the wall on either side of her, trapping her. "What are you doing?" His voice was deep and sexy.

"Get out of my way. I have to get to William."

Harrison didn't move. His masculine aroma enveloped her, and she marveled that she could smell in this dream. "No, you don't."

Panic rose in her chest. "Yes, I do! He needs me."

"*I* need you, Penny." Harrison looked in her eyes. "William isn't real. But I am." He pressed closer, until her heart pounded against his solid chest. "You like kissing me. Admit it."

And then his lips were on hers, and fire spread through her. No. She shouldn't enjoy kissing Harrison. William needed her. But she didn't stop kissing Harrison. His lips were too warm, too tantalizing. Kissing him was like tasting heaven. And she wanted more. Then his lips were on her cheek, her jaw line, her ear lobe.

"Please, stop." She could barely get the words out. She had to fight with all her will power.

"I won't stop until you admit it," he whispered in her ear.

"Okay, I admit it," Why was it so hard to talk in this dream? It was like she had a mouth full of marshmallows. "I like kissing you."

He smiled. "I knew it."

Then he vanished.

Penny awoke to sunlight streaming in from the sliding glass door. She blinked and the sight of Harrison, lying in the recliner, came into view and she realized he was staring at her. "Good morning."

"Mmmm." She rolled over and threw the covers over her head. Why did she have to wake from that dream? It was so realistic. And she could have kissed the imaginary Harrison all day. She groaned. "Not really."

He laughed. "What were you dreaming about?"

"Why? What did I do?"

"You were talking in your sleep."

Terror shot through her. No. She hadn't, had she? Was that why it was so hard to speak? She slowly turned to face him, afraid of what the answer would be, but needing to ask. "What did I say?"

He grinned. "Nothing much."

She blew out a breath of relief. Thank goodness. The last

thing she needed was for Harrison to think she enjoyed kissing him. No matter what she dreamed about, she loved William and needed to work things out with him.

Harrison pushed down the footrest and stood. "Guess I'd better go shower. I have to be in the office in an hour."

A new kind of panic arose in her and she sat up, clutching the covers. "What? You're leaving me?"

He tossed his blanket on the chair. "I can't ignore my job, Penny."

"So I'm stuck here. With *her*. That's just great. What am I supposed to do all day?"

A puzzled look crossed his face. "You're not stuck here. Antonio will take you wherever you want to go."

Penny couldn't understand why he wasn't getting it. "And where would I go? I don't know anyone here. Except William. Wait. Do you think Antonio would take me to—"

"No." His voice was firm. "You're not going to meet William without me there. End of discussion."

"End of discussion? Did you really just say that to me?" Heat flushed to her face and she ground her teeth.

"That's not what I meant." His voice softened. "I'm just worried about you."

She blew out a frustrated breath and fell back onto the pillows. "Fine. I'll just stay in this room, then."

"Don't be ridiculous." He crossed the room to the closet. "There's enough house here, I'm sure you could find something to do without running into her."

"Well I'm not sure I want to find out."

He disappeared into the closet, but his voice carried. "Just don't embarrass her in front of her friends and you'll be fine."

"I think I embarrass her just by being here."

He emerged with a suit in hand, and chuckled. "That might be true."

She moaned and covered her face with her hands. "I'm going to be stuck here. Like a prisoner."

His laugh came from the bathroom. "Such drama. Would you rather come to work with me?"

Anything would be better than being stuck in the house with the Wicked Witch of the West. "Yes!" She hopped out of bed. "Yes, please. Take me to work with you."

"All right. There's another shower in the room next door. We'll leave in thirty minutes."

~

Patrice made sure no one was watching as she slipped out the back door and headed toward the garage. She made her way up the apartment steps and knocked on the door. Antonio peeked out.

"It's all there." She handed him an envelope.

He nodded and took it from her. "Thank you."

A noise from the trees startled her and she jumped around. A bird fluttered and flew off into the sky. "I'd better go."

"See you tonight then?" His eyes held hope.

She nodded. "After midnight."

CHAPTER 10

Harrison gazed out of his large office window. The city stretched out before him in a spectacular view, but his mind wasn't on the scenery. How long had Penny been talking to that nitwit over in sales, thirty minutes? Forty? He looked at the clock again. Nope, it had only been twenty-one minutes. Still, every once in a while he could hear her laughter carry down the hallway to his office. What was that guy's name? Franklin. Right. Same name as that cartoon turtle. He even looked like a turtle. A short neck, hunched shoulders, and hardly any hair. Why was Penny talking to him, anyway?

He bounced his leg and shuffled the papers on his desk. Bringing her to work had been a bad idea. She'd sat on one of the leather chairs in his office, her legs crossed, reading a copy of Pride and Prejudice she'd taken from his stepmother's library and distracting him from getting any work done. Then she'd wandered down the hall, to go exploring as she put it, and was now talking to Turtle Man.

Her laughter sounded once again and Harrison stood abruptly, forcing his chair to shoot backward and bump against the wall. What on earth were they talking about? He stalked down the hall to Franklin's office and stuck his head in.

Penny was partially sitting on the edge of the desk, one foot on the floor. "I know. David Tennant was my favorite, too."

"I can't believe they killed off Amy. She was the bomb." Franklin put his hand near Penny's knee and Harrison wanted to waltz in and rip the guy's little turtle head off.

Harrison cleared his throat.

Penny turned toward the door. "Oh, hi. Franklin and I were just talking. He watches *Doctor Who*, too."

"That's great. I was wondering…" He looked at his watch. Eleven. A little early for lunch, but he couldn't think of any other excuse as to why he needed her. "Do you want to go grab a bite to eat?"

Penny hopped off the desk. "Sure."

The closer she got to him, the less he wanted to kill Franklin. He snaked his arm around her waist. It felt right. "Chinese sound okay?"

She tossed him one of her bright smiles. "Great."

As he walked with her out to his Maserati, he marveled at how good she looked in her jeans and a T-shirt sporting the saying, "There's a fine line between numerator and denominator." Most people would look frumpy, but she somehow pulled it off.

He slid into his seat and clicked his seatbelt. "I know this great little mom and pop place. It's a little out of the way, but they have the best egg rolls."

"I don't mind out of the way." Her smile turned sheepish. "I was getting a little bored. A road trip with you sounds nice."

Did she just say she wanted to spend time with him? And why did that thought please him so much? He turned on the radio and eased the car onto the freeway. "Feel free to change the station if you'd like."

"No, I don't mind the oldies channel."

Heat crept up his neck to his ears. She'd caught him listening to the 80's station. Oh well. At least she liked it. He gripped the steering wheel and sped up. A Whitney Houston song came on and Penny started singing along.

He listened for a minute, in awe of her voice. In fact, he'd never known anyone who could sing so well. She was tackling the song like it was nothing. "I didn't know you could sing."

She stopped and gave him a sideways glance. "I told you I was a performer."

He hated to admit it, but he'd dismissed it as being another one of her crazy ideas. He was amazed she actually had talent. "You're good."

"Thanks."

"Have you ever performed anywhere?" Why hadn't he asked her that before?

"Yes. I had a small part in a Las Vegas show. That's why I was living there. Unfortunately, it didn't last, so I was stuck there working at the coffee shop, trying to find something else. It was yet another thing that my father told me wouldn't work out, and he was right. It didn't." She blew her hair out of her face and stared out the window.

"I'm sure your father means well."

"He does. I just wish I could have succeeded and proven him wrong."

The look on her face was so downhearted, it stirred a desperate urge in him to cheer her up. "You got a part in a Las Vegas show. I bet not every aspiring performer can say that."

Her lips lifted in a partial smile. "You're right."

"And I'm sure many artists have failures and setbacks before their careers take off."

"Yes. You're right again." She patted his leg. "I just wish my father would understand."

"What does he want you to do?"

"Something safe. Boring. Like accounting."

He chuckled. "Well, if your shirt is any indication, you do like math."

"I like math jokes. Not quite the same thing." She twisted her hands together. "Plus, I have this other talent, besides singing, I mean. It's stupid, really, but Dad thinks I should use it in my career."

Harrison pulled off the freeway and merged into the traffic. "What is it?"

"I can do math in my head."

"Can't everyone?"

"No, I mean I can do really complicated math in my head." She turned away, like she was embarrassed.

"Isn't that a good thing?"

"Not really. It intimidates most people, so I try not to bring it up." She looked down at her hands.

The Chinese restaurant came into view, so he changed lanes and pulled into the parking lot. "Why would you being able to do math in your head intimidate people?"

She shrugged. "It just does."

"That's ridiculous."

She arched an eyebrow, like he'd challenged her so she needed to prove him wrong. "Ask me anything."

"What's twelve times twelve?"

She rolled her eyes. "Everyone knows that. You're not even trying."

He didn't want to admit that he wasn't sure what the answer was, so he laughed. "Okay, okay. What's one hundred, twenty-three times sixteen?"

She looked up and to the left, like she was calculating it out in her mind. "One thousand, nine-hundred, sixty-eight."

Since he had no idea if she was right, he pulled out his phone and opened his calculator app. "Nice. Okay, here's a harder one." He typed in a random number. "One thousand, seven hundred, sixty-two divided by fifty-one." He hit the equal button and immediately regretted just making something up. The answer had a decimal point with a long string of numbers.

Again, she looked up, but waited a little longer this time.

"Never mind. That was too hard."

"Well, it's thirty-four point five four nine zero one nine, but I'm going to need another second if you want it divided out further."

His mouth fell open. "Six. That's the only one left. How did you—?"

"No," she said, still looking up. "It goes further. Your calculator just rounded. It's six zero seven eight four three one four."

Harrison stared at her. "How do you know that?"

Her cheeks turned pink. "Like I said, I can do math in my head."

He didn't want to admit it, but she was right. That was intimidating. He forced a laugh. "Well, I know who's calculating the tip."

She smiled, her eyes hopeful. "You don't feel threatened?"

He did, but he shook his head. "Not at all. You're good at math. I can throw stuff together and make awesome omelets. Everyone has their strengths."

Her smile widened. "Good. I was afraid I was going to make you feel weird."

Inadequate, unintelligent, dumb. Those were the words swirling around in his head. But he ignored it. "Nah. Let's go in and eat."

𝒫enny followed Harrison into the restaurant with the smell of ginger thick in the air. Two red dragons faced each other in a huge painting on the wall. The noise of people chatting and dishes clinking carried through the establishment. A woman showed them to their seats.

"I suggest the lunch buffet." Harrison smiled like he was about to share a secret.

"You come here often?"

He nodded. "As often as I can. I haven't been in a while. Busy at work." A quick frown crossed his face but in a second it was gone.

After they filled their plates and sat back down, Penny decided to broach the subject she'd been thinking about all morning. "I know you're busy with work, and this might not be a great time, but I was wondering if we could go to Santa Barbara this evening."

Harrison slowly finished chewing his food. He lowered his fork. "Did William agree to meet with you?"

She pushed a cashew around on her plate. "No."

"Then what do you have in mind?"

That was the problem. She didn't know what she had in mind. Show up on his doorstep? The thought had been shoving its way into her brain. "I don't know."

Harrison wiped the corner of his mouth with his napkin. "I don't think we should surprise him by knocking on his door."

"What if we were to accidentally run into him? Like at the grocery store?"

"You mean, go sit outside his house and wait for him to leave and then follow him, trying to be discreet, so we can bump into him in a normal public setting?"

She grinned. "Great idea!"

He scowled and leaned back in his chair. "I was being sarcastic. That's a terrible idea."

She was afraid of that. "Darn."

"You should really talk to him more before going all the way out there to meet with him, anyway."

"What does that mean?"

He wouldn't look her in the eye. "Just that you should ask him what he's not telling you."

Anger built up in her like a pressure cooker about to blow. "What did you do?"

Guilt showed on his face as plain as the pool of soy sauce on her plate. "Nothing."

"You did! You checked him out online!"

As soon as she said it, his face confirmed it.

"I can't believe you." She folded her arms across her chest and hunched into the back of her chair. He was way out of line. What business of his was it, anyway? And who cares what he thinks he found out. It wasn't important. She glared at the floor.

William told her everything. Whatever Harrison found out, she probably already knew. Didn't she? There couldn't be anything William was hiding. They had an open and honest relationship. Even if they hadn't met in person yet.

She chanced a glance at Harrison. He looked like one of those dog shaming photos she'd seen on Facebook. It almost made her feel guilty for yelling at him.

He was just trying to help, anyway. She shouldn't be so hard on him. And he must have learned something or he wouldn't have been urging her to talk to William.

Curiosity wormed its way into her. What had he found out? Was there something William was keeping from her? She didn't want to ask, but the words flew out of her mouth anyway. "What did you find out?"

He shook his head. "Oh, no. I'm not getting in the middle

of whatever it is you guys have going on. I'm keeping my mouth shut."

And of course, that made her want to know even more. "Just tell me."

"No."

She huffed. "Fine. I'll just get on your computer and look."

Harrison blanched, then squirmed in his seat. "He's married."

CHAPTER 11

The restaurant melted around her, like someone had poured hot water on a wax painting. Her throat constricted and breathing became difficult.

"Penny? Are you okay?"

She knew it was Harrison's voice, but everything seemed muffled, and her head spun.

"Penny. Breathe." Harrison squeezed her shoulders and she realized he was behind her. "It's okay. You're going to be fine."

The room grew impossibly hot. She needed air. Had to get out of there. She stumbled out of her chair and sprinted toward the door. December in L.A. wasn't cold like back home in Iowa, but the 70 degree breeze felt cool on her skin and she leaned up against the building and gulped in the fresh air.

The door opened and Harrison rushed to her side, concern etching a frown on his face. "You okay?"

She shook her head. "I don't think so."

His arms wrapped around her and the musky smell of his

cologne enveloped her. She buried her head in his shoulder as sobs wracked her body.

Harrison didn't say "I told you so," or "You stupid girl," like she was sure he was thinking. Instead, he simply held her while the traffic sped by and her heart shattered into tiny pieces. He rubbed small circles on her back.

When she'd gathered her composure, she pulled away. "How could I have been so stupid?"

"Hush, now. You're far from stupid." He kissed her forehead, and her heart sped up. "You are the most loving, kind, and generous person I know. He tried to take advantage of you."

"But, I should have seen. Should have known."

"How? Did he ever give you any indication he was married?"

She stared at the concrete. "No."

Harrison lifted her chin and forced her to look into his eyes. Two deep pools of blue met her gaze, and her knees grew weak. He had the most amazing eyes. Why hadn't she noticed before? His thumb grazed her jawline, which added to the weak knee thing. "You are trusting. And loyal. It wasn't your fault."

Conflicting emotions surged. Anger, hurt, and betrayal for what William had done. And something else she couldn't name, but it emerged as she looked into Harrison's blue eyes. She turned away. "I was naïve."

"Yes." He moved his hands to her shoulders. "That's one of the many appealing things about you."

Frustration welled inside her and she blew out a breath. "Ugh. How could I have forgiven him for leaving me at the altar? Why did I listen to him?"

"Because you care. And you've given him your heart. It's hard to walk away from a relationship, even an online one, when you've put your heart into it." He paused, and his gaze landed on her lips. The moment suddenly turned more personal, and her breath caught.

Was he about to kiss her? She searched his eyes.

He blinked and took a step back. "Maybe we should go to Santa Barbara tonight. In fact, I can take the rest of the day off. We'll go to a coffee shop and you can text him. Since he's married, he won't appreciate you showing up on his doorstep. Maybe he'll meet you somewhere public. I think you need to talk."

Being on the emotional roller coaster left her drained. Harrison was right. She had to break it off with William, face to face. Confront him about his wife. Let him know things were over. Maybe get rid of her cell phone so he couldn't text her anymore. She was overdue on the bill anyway. "Okay."

He put his arm around her shoulders and led her back through the restaurant. After he paid the bill, they left.

She sat in the car, numb. How long had William been married? Did he meet his wife during her relationship with him? Or had he been married for quite some time? She had to know. "What date was on the marriage license?"

Harrison's jaw clenched and he stared out the windshield. "I don't think you want to go there, Penny."

Did she? The question festered in her mind. "Tell me. I need to know."

Harrison sighed. "If I refuse to tell you, you'll just go look it up anyway, won't you?"

"Yes."

He was silent for a minute, and it was obvious he didn't want to say it. "He got married fifteen years ago."

"*Fifteen years?*" She tried not to shout, but it didn't work. "I was ten. How old is he?"

From the pained expression on Harrison's face, Penny knew it wasn't good news. When he didn't say anything, she repeated herself. "How old, Harrison?"

"Forty."

Penny felt another panic attack come on. "Are you kidding me? He's forty?"

His pained expression didn't go away. If anything, it got worse.

Penny gaped. "What else is there? You're not telling me everything."

"Remember the photo he sent?"

No. This wasn't happening. Everything she knew about him was a lie. "Was that someone else's photo?"

"Not exactly."

She pulled out her phone and flipped to the photo. "What about it?"

"He's not the blurry one."

A lump formed in her throat. "You mean he's the short bald guy in back?"

Harrison sent her an apologetic look. "Sorry. You almost married Danny Devito."

~

Harrison stretched out in the corner booth of All Ground Up. He'd agreed to keep his distance and let them talk alone. Penny seemed nervous, wringing her hands and looking out the front window, sitting at a table waiting for him to arrive. She'd ordered a lemonade, which she occasionally sipped. The coffee she'd ordered for William sat, untouched. Lively Christmas piano music played over the speakers.

When she'd first texted William, he hadn't wanted to meet. Harrison clenched his teeth. The jerk apparently wanted to string her along forever. But once he found out Penny was already in town, less than three miles from his house, he'd changed his mind. She hadn't told him Harrison had come as well.

He picked up his bagel and took a bite. Not bad. The walnut cream cheese spread was pretty good. He chased it down with a swig of his coffee.

This booth was perfect because it offered Penny a little privacy – he couldn't hear their conversation. But it gave him a good view in case William got upset about the breakup. Not knowing his temperament, Harrison didn't want to be too far. He could get to Penny in two seconds.

The bell jingled and his gaze traveled to the door. William. He was taller than he looked in his photo, but just as bald. He immediately spotted Penny and turned on what he probably thought was a charming smile. Harrison scowled.

Penny stood and gave him a hug, which surprised Harrison. Wasn't she there to tell him off? Give it a final break? Kick him in the tuckus and send him packing? The whole reason he'd suggested the meeting was so she could have closure and move on.

William pulled out the chair for Penny and Harrison groaned. Was he trying to be a gentleman, after all he'd done? Was there no end to this guy's delusion?

As they sat and talked, Penny grew emotional. She dabbed at her eyes with her napkin. William reached across the table and took her hands in his. What was he saying? Penny nodded, blinked again, and wiped another tear. What Harrison wouldn't give to be able to read lips.

∽

*P*enny drew in a breath and tried to remain calm. She knew this man, even if some of the details had been wrong. His heart was the same. But he needed to answer some hard questions. "Why didn't you tell me you were married?"

William's face fell, and he stared down at the table. "I'm sorry. It ended almost three years ago. She just won't sign the divorce papers."

That was possible. Penny narrowed her eyes. "Ended...as in how?"

He shrugged. "She left me. Just packed up her stuff and ran off with the dog groomer. We've been separated ever since."

Wow. She wasn't expecting such a good answer. It was almost believable. In fact, she found herself *wanting* to believe him. She didn't want to think the last two years had been a total lie. "Why won't she sign the papers?"

He exhaled and his shoulders slumped, the perfect impression of a beaten man. "I don't know. Because I want them signed? I think she's trying to punish me."

The sadness in his eyes stabbed at her heart. Sure, he wasn't a hunk like Harrison. But she knew he had a beautiful soul. It wasn't fair for his estranged wife to do that to him. "Can't you do something about it?"

"I was hoping she would sign the papers on her own." He picked up his coffee and took a sip. "I guess that's not going to work."

Penny traced the lid on her lemonade. If what he was saying was true, and it did make sense, then why didn't he just tell her? The fact that he had hidden his marriage hurt more than anything. "I can't believe you kept something like that from me." Tears threatened to spill down her cheeks again, so she blinked them back.

His gaze met hers, the pain in his eyes clear. "I'm so sorry. I was hoping to take care of it and not have to bother you with it. Your suggestion to get married threw me off."

What? Penny gaped at William. "*My* suggestion? That was *your* bright idea."

"It was?" His brow wrinkled. "Well, I don't remember the details. I just know I wanted to." He took her hands in his. "I fell in love with you, even though we'd never met. I know it sounds ridiculous, but that's what happened."

"It happened to me, too."

William smiled and sat back in his chair, like that solved everything, which annoyed her. He wasn't getting off that easy. Penny frowned. "I know we connected on a personal level in our conversations, but you were lying to me. You didn't even tell me your real age."

His smile faded and he ran his hand over his bald head. "I'm sorry. When I sent you that photo you thought I was Blake. I was going to say something, but you went on and on about how handsome I was, and how we'd make a great couple, and I couldn't correct you. I wasn't sure we'd ever meet in real life anyway."

"'Wasn't sure?' You kept asking me to run away for a weekend with you."

He grinned, which looked more like a leer. "The offer is still open."

She suddenly wanted to stuff her lemonade so far down his throat it would come out the other side. Clenching her fists, she said, "You aren't even listening to me."

"That's not true. You love me. I love you. We have some problems, but those can be worked out. Why should we be apart now because of some minor details?"

"You being married is *not* a minor detail!" She clamped her hand over her mouth when she realized she was shouting. Everyone in the coffee shop looked at them. She lowered her voice. "You can't sweep that under the rug."

"I'll talk to my ex. Get her to sign the papers. Please, just give us a chance. I'll get plane tickets. We could go somewhere private this weekend and get to know each other better." Desperation filled his eyes, and Penny realized she'd never even known him at all.

"You make me sick."

She was about to stand when a brunette walked by, stopped, and did a double take. "William? I thought that was you. Are we still on for tonight?"

The panicked expression on his face told Penny everything. William glanced between the two of them. "I…uh…"

A seductive smile formed on the woman's face. "Call me." Her hips swayed as she left the coffee shop.

William turned to her with wide eyes. "That wasn't what it looked like."

Penny gripped her lemonade so tight the lid popped off. How could she have been fooled by this man? Disgust filled her and she tossed the contents of her cup in his face.

His mouth opened as cold lemonade splashed him and dripped down his shirt.

"Don't text me again," Penny said between clenched teeth.

Harrison appeared by her side. "Everything okay?"

She stood. "Yes. We're done here." She grabbed Harrison's arm and dragged him outside.

He bit his lip in an obvious attempt not to laugh. "What happened?"

"Ugh!" She stormed up the sidewalk to where his car was parked, the afternoon sun casting long shadows. "I don't want to talk about it."

"No problem." He unlocked the car and opened her door for her.

She slid in. "I can't believe him! What a colossal jerk."

Harrison got behind the wheel. "I thought you didn't want to talk about it."

"Shut up."

He pulled out into traffic.

"He's seeing someone else! Not only did the jerk lie about being married, he's got another girl on the side."

"Ouch. I'm sorry." He shot her a sympathetic glance.

"I can't believe I wasted two years chatting with him online, believing his lies." Her hands shook and blood pounded in her ears. Her phone screamed, "Text Message!" She rolled down the window and tossed her cell out, watching it fly into pieces in the side view mirror.

The shock on Harrison's face was clear. "Well. At least you didn't find out after you married him."

The thought made her shiver. "Yeah. I'd be in jail right now."

He turned, his eyebrow raised. "Jail?"

"I'm no good at hiding bodies."

CHAPTER 12

A sliver of bright light came through the curtains, slicing across the bed. Penny knew she should get up. Maybe take a shower. But the thought of moving didn't appeal to her. Her life stunk.

She'd wasted so much time on William. The sleazebag. She should have known. He'd always wanted to take her somewhere, away for a weekend. How transparent was that? Of course he was married. She was the other woman. Arg. It sounded so terrible. Pain seared through her chest. She pulled her pillow over her head and closed her eyes. How did her life get so far into the toilet?

The bedroom door clicked open and footsteps sounded across the hardwood floor. Big footsteps. Must be Harrison. She didn't care. The curtains rustled and light poured in. "Okay, time to get out of bed." Harrison's deep voice filled the room.

She moaned, but peeked out from under the pillow anyway.

Harrison stood by the bed, his fists on his hips, a stance

her mother used to take when she meant business, although she usually had a rolling pin in her hand and an apron on.

Penny suppressed a smile. "I don't want to."

"You can't wallow in self-pity forever. Get up. You haven't gotten out of bed for days."

"I have too."

A skeptical look crossed his face.

"I have!"

He picked up an empty container of Ben and Jerry's sitting on the night stand. "Going downstairs to get ice cream from the kitchen doesn't count." He tossed it in the trash, where it landed among mounds of tissues. "Now get up and take a shower. We're going out."

She wrinkled her nose. She didn't want to go anywhere. Didn't want to have this conversation. Just wanted to crawl back under the covers. "No thanks."

He frowned and put his hands behind his back. "I thought you might be difficult, so I bought these." He pulled out two tickets and waved them in the air, like they would suddenly make her want to jump out of bed.

"Nice try." She buried her head in a pillow. "I don't feel like going anywhere."

"Not even to…" He held the tickets close to his face. "ElfCon?"

If he had said he wanted to dance naked on the ceiling, it wouldn't have shocked her more. "ElfCon? Are you serious?" She sat up. "You really have tickets to ElfCon?"

He swiped the tickets away and rocked back on his heels. "If I did, would you get out of bed and go with me?"

"Are you freakin' kidding me?"

"I heard Martin Freeman was going to be there." He smiled like he'd just eaten the cat. Or something like that. She couldn't think straight at the moment.

She hopped out of bed and rushed at him, trying to grab

the tickets. He held them too far away for her to reach. "Some other dude is going to be there. Some guy named—"

"Benedict Cumberbatch, I know! Give them!"

He laughed as she pulled his arm down and grabbed the tickets. They really did say ElfCon. And they weren't just admission tickets. They were premium passes that got them into the panel discussion. "No freakin' way!"

He laughed again. "I thought that would pull you out of your funk."

She glared at him. "I wasn't in a *funk*." The bed bounced as she plopped down. "I was trying to decide if life was worth living."

He turned serious, and sat next to her. "Is it?"

She took a deep breath and exhaled, staring at her lap. William was a liar. She'd wasted a lot of time on him. He'd hurt her more than she wanted to admit. But Harrison knew. She looked up into his amazing blue eyes. He'd gone to a lot of trouble to make her feel better. He didn't care two snits about ElfCon. He'd only gotten the tickets because she loved that kind of thing. "Yeah. It is."

He took her in a one-arm hug, and electricity zinged through her. "Good. Now you'd better go shower. You smell awful."

She shoved him.

He fell over on the bed, laughing.

"You meanie."

He stood and crossed the room. "I almost forgot." He opened the door and grabbed something hanging on the handle. His cheeks turned pink. "I got this for you."

She stared at the most beautiful blue elven dress she'd ever seen, complete with flowing bell sleeves and matching cloak. The squeal just came out. "Eeeeeee! I love it!"

"I heard this was appropriate attire for something like ElfCon."

"It's perfect." She eyed him. "But what will you wear?'

A small smile played on his lips. "You'll see."

∽

Harrison felt like an idiot. He paced the front hall, waiting for Penny to come down the curved staircase, trying not to step on his cloak. At least the leather boots were comfortable.

Trent walked in and stopped short. "What the…?"

Harrison scowled. "I know. You don't have to say it."

The stunned look on Trent's face turned into a smirk. "Are you wearing a tunic?"

"I'm taking Penny to ElfCon. And by all means, go ahead and laugh, because you obviously want to."

Trent chuckled. "Man. If I didn't know any better, I'd say you had it bad for her."

Did he? He wasn't sure. He turned away, not wanting to be badgered by his younger brother.

"Wait." Trent grabbed Harrison's arm, forcing him to look at his face. "You've got to be kidding me. You've fallen for this girl?"

"Don't be ridiculous. She's a means to an end."

Trent's eyes narrowed. "Uh, huh."

From the look on his face, it was clear Trent didn't believe him. He wasn't even sure he believed himself. But before he had a chance to figure out his own feelings, he didn't want anyone jumping to the wrong conclusions. Exasperated, he blurted, "I'm just trying to cheer her up after she found out the man she was supposed to marry was cheating on her."

Trent stepped back. "Ouch."

"Yes. She's very upset. So please, be nice to her."

His face turned contemplative. "This thing you're doing. It's so unlike you."

Harrison folded his arms across his chest. "It will take her mind off—"

"No, not the ElfCon. I mean, this whole marriage-over-the-weekend thing." Trent studied him. "I'm usually the one to run off and do crazy things. You're the Harvard graduate. The reliable one."

Trent was right. Harrison had been born to fill a role, and he'd never strayed from it. It was his duty to take over his father's business. He was to carry on the legacy of the Williams name. While his brother, on the other hand, didn't know the meaning of hard work. "Unlike you."

Trent scowled, but he didn't say anything. Instead, he turned to look out the window.

Avoidance. He was good at that. Trent had dropped out of college, married to get his share of the trust fund, and now spent his time playing video games and hanging around the mansion. Harrison wasn't sure when Trent would mature and decide what he wanted to be when he grew up.

Trent continued to stare out the window. "Yeah. Unlike me."

"I didn't mean—I just—don't you want to do anything with your life?"

"Maybe I can work at the firm."

Harrison's mouth dropped open. "You want to work at the company?"

Trent turned and leaned against the staircase. "I don't know. There's got to be something I can do there."

Harrison had never imagined Trent would want to work at the firm. He'd always been aloof when the topic had been discussed. But it was a family business. He supposed he could try to find something for him to do. "Why don't you come in on Monday? We'll see where we can put you."

Trent pushed off the banister and headed down the hall. "Okay," he said in that nonchalant way he always had.

How long would Trent last "working" for the corporation? Harrison wasn't positive. But surely he could find something for him to do that wouldn't totally screw up everything.

"What was that about?" Penny's voice startled him, and he turned to see her at the top of the staircase. Her strawberry blonde hair cascaded down her shoulders in ringlets. The dress he'd purchased fit her perfectly. She looked like a medieval goddess. She lifted her skirt and started down the steps, her sparkling blue shoes peeking out from the material.

"Nothing." All thoughts of Trent were gone. He couldn't take his gaze off her.

"You look nice." Her eyes held a smile.

He'd forgotten he was dressed like some 13th century woodsman. "Are you ready to go, milady?" He held out his arm.

"You betcha."

∼

ElfCon was everything Penny had expected and more. The costumes were fun. Harrison had obviously spent a lot on theirs, because they looked so authentic that several people stopped them and asked if they could take their picture. Harrison put up with it in good humor. In fact, she was amazed at how well he tolerated the whole experience. He went to each booth with her, stood in line to get autographs, and even sat through the panel discussion without scowling. When Penny wanted to join in on a role playing game, he sat beside her and acted interested in it.

The hurt from William's deception didn't disappear, but

ElfCon took her mind off it. Being with the most handsome man at the convention helped, too. For some reason, he looked extra sexy in his Legolas costume. Not that she would tell him. His ego couldn't handle it.

Just as they were about to leave, Penny heard someone call out to her. She turned and there was Josephine, dressed in a tight leather cat woman costume and tremendous heels. It was a far cry from the look she'd worn last week: old lady going to tea.

Penny choked out a greeting. "Josephine. What are you doing here?"

The woman, who had to be pushing eighty, smiled and took Penny's hand. "I come every year, dear. Wouldn't miss it. I love this stuff. And look at you two. I didn't know Harrison was into this scene."

Penny glanced at him. He appeared to be trying to pull his tongue off the floor and back in his mouth. She answered for him. "He's not. It's my thing."

For her age, she looked pretty good in the costume. Josephine looped her arm through Penny's. "Well, isn't he a good husband?"

The phrase slapped Penny across the face, and she stared at Josephine. Of course, they were pretending to be married. Or, rather, they *were* married. And to an outsider, it would look like Harrison was being a good husband. In fact, he was going above and beyond their agreement. He didn't have to bring her to ElfCon. They weren't there playing a role. He'd done it because…

Why had he done it?

She wasn't quite sure. Maybe he'd gotten tired of her sulking in bed. That had to be it. He needed her up and around so they looked like a real married couple. The possibility of it being anything else was absurd.

"Yes, he is," she finally said.

Josephine tugged her along the corridor, and Penny was amazed at the agility with which the old woman managed those heels. "You are coming to my soirée tomorrow, aren't you?"

Crud. She'd forgotten about that. She looked to Harrison for help, but he simply smiled at her. She finally settled on, "Um, I don't know."

Josephine frowned. "You can't miss it, dear. Everyone will be there."

"I don't think I have anything to wear."

A bright look came on Josephine's face. "Then we shall go shopping in the morning!"

Harrison didn't object. In fact he folded his arms across his chest and smiled. "Good idea."

Penny wasn't sure if she should be excited or nervous. "Okay, then I guess we're going."

CHAPTER 13

Penny lay in bed, the events of the day playing in her head. Harrison had really stepped up to the plate. He'd been the perfect gentleman, trying hard to get into the things she liked. He'd even purchased a TARDIS paper weight for his office. How cute was that?

And now, all she could do was listen to his even breathing and wonder what it would be like to really be married to him. Stupid. She was nothing like the kind of women who lived around here. She'd never fit into his world. And what made her think he wanted her to? Because he'd been nice to her today?

She punched her pillow and rolled over. Such dumb thinking. She needed to clear her head. Wasn't she fooling herself about William not three days ago? What did she know about relationships? She needed to get away from men for a while. Think about her future.

Harrison's soft voice broke into her thoughts. "You awake too?"

She jumped, her heart pounding. She'd thought he was

asleep. Thank goodness she hadn't been talking to herself. "Yeah. Can't sleep."

He sat the recliner upright. "How about a midnight snack?"

"Now you're talking."

She slipped out of bed and padded to the door. Only after she entered the hallway did she turn to look at him. He was wearing striped pajama pants and a cotton T-shirt that hugged his chest.

She tried not to stare at his muscles as the two of them snuck down to the kitchen. Really. No one should look that good. It was doing things to her head. The skin on his arms looked smooth. She pushed back a ridiculous urge to touch it.

He pulled open the fridge and scanned the contents. "How about I whip us up some guacamole? Does that sound good?" His muscles bulged as he turned to look at her.

She forced her eyes away from him. "Sure."

Harrison pulled out two ripe avocados and went to work gathering ingredients, utensils, and a bowl. Penny watched him as he cut the avocados and sprinkled cumin and other spices in. It was clear he loved what he was doing. The smile never left his face. She wanted to mention it, but things had gotten tense last time, so she let it go.

After he was done, he pulled out a bag of corn chips and dumped them in a bowl. "You want to go first?" He motioned to the concoction.

She picked up a chip and scooped up a generous portion. It looked delicious and tasted even better. "Mmm." She closed her eyes and savored the flavor. When she opened them again she was surprised to find Harrison staring at her, a look she couldn't quite interpret on his face. "What?"

He smiled, the look disappearing. "Nothing. I'm glad you like it."

They ate in silence for a few minutes, but it didn't feel uncomfortable. Penny rather liked his presence. His smile put her at ease.

She scraped the bowl with the last chip. "So, what's up with your brother? Why's he always hanging around here?"

Harrison lifted one shoulder. "I'm not sure. If I had to guess, I'd say he can't stand his wife."

"Oh no. I didn't know they weren't happy. How long have they been together?"

He waved his hand in a nonchalant way. "I don't think they're really 'together'," he said, using air quotes. "It's another business arrangement. I mean, he hasn't come out and admitted it, but all things point to it."

Penny's mouth fell open and she had to force it closed. "What is up with you people? Don't you believe in falling in love and marrying for real?"

Harrison's intense blue eyes focused on her. "I used to."

He said it so softly she could barely hear him, and the pain behind his eyes made her recoil. Of course. That was why Carol's betrayal had hurt him so much. "I'm sorry, I didn't mean—"

He held up a hand. "Don't. It's okay."

She fiddled with the cheap metal ring still on her finger. "I guess we've both been disillusioned."

The mood in the room darkened, and Harrison stood. "Yeah." He picked up the bowl and took it to the sink.

After they cleaned up the kitchen, they went back to bed, neither one saying anything.

~

Morning came too quickly. After showering and getting dressed, Penny waited at the window by the front door. Josephine roared up into the circular driveway in a bright pink Lamborghini and jerked to a stop. She rolled down the passenger window and called out. "Are you ready, dear?"

Penny slid into the seat and closed the door, not knowing quite what to expect from a morning out shopping with Josephine. "As ready as I'll ever be."

The older woman gunned the car. "We're going to have so much fun!"

Penny gave her a sly smile. "We sure are." She held up the credit card Harrison had given her. Josephine's cackle filled the air and warmed Penny's heart.

The drive didn't last too long. Soon they were entering a swanky store filled with designer dresses. Penny tried not to pay attention to the prices, but when Josephine pulled out a little black thing with a thousand dollar tag, Penny choked. "There's hardly anything to this. I'm not paying a thousand dollars for a glorified slip."

Josephine laughed. "Okay. Nothing too revealing then." She slid the hanger back on the rack and ushered Penny over to another area with floor length gowns.

As they looked through them, Penny's eyes started to glaze over. How could she pick one? They were all so gorgeous. And each price tag seemed to outdo the last. She swallowed the lump forming in her throat.

Josephine held up a stunning emerald green dress with jewels sewn in to accent the neckline and waist.

It actually made Penny gasp.

Josephine gave her a knowing look. "This is it, isn't it?"

Penny chewed her bottom lip. "It's breathtaking. But I'm not sure it's...right for me."

A frown formed on Josephine's face. "What's wrong with it?"

One flip of the tag revealed the three-thousand-dollar price. "This."

"Nonsense." Josephine frowned and flipped her hand. "Surely Harrison can afford it."

Maybe. But would he think she was being excessive? What if he told her it was coming out of her part of the money? There was no way she could afford to spend three thousand on something so frivolous. She needed that money for important things, like food and shelter. "I think we'd better look in a different store."

Josephine scoffed and pulled out her phone. She spoke for a minute, then hung up and started toward the dressing rooms. "He says not to worry about it. Let's see how it looks on you."

Penny reluctantly followed, feeling guilty for even thinking about trying on the dress. Even though Harrison had money, it wasn't fair for her to spend it. Not when they weren't really a couple. She tried to smile as Josephine shoved her into one of the stalls.

No matter how she felt about it, Josephine wasn't going to let her off the hook, so Penny undressed. She slipped the gown on and fumbled with the zipper for a moment before succeeding. She turned to the mirror and stared, mouth open. The dress made her look like a queen, hugging her in all the right places.

Josephine's voice carried over the stall. "Come on out. I want to see." Then she banged on the door for emphasis.

Knowing she couldn't get out of it, Penny opened the door. Josephine shrieked and motioned for Penny to turn around. "Wow girl, this is the dress. Look how it brings out the green in your eyes. You look amazing. That husband of yours won't be able to keep his hands off you."

Penny doubted that would be an issue, but pressed her lips together to keep from saying it. Instead she smiled and looked to the floor. "Thank you."

Josephine flipped her wrist and glanced at a jewel studded

watch. "Okay. Let's hurry. We still need to find some shoes that match, and I've got to get back to make sure the caterer knows where to set things up."

Resigning to Josephine's will, Penny changed back into her clothes and purchased the crazy expensive but amazingly gorgeous dress.

CHAPTER 14

Harrison pulled his car into the long circular drive. The home was decorated with thousands of little white Christmas lights. It was a beautiful sight.

A young man jogged over to him. Of course Josephine would have valet parking. He rolled his eyes, but handed his keys over. Josephine didn't do anything halfway, did she? He rushed to the passenger side of the car and opened the door for Penny.

For the second time that night, the sight of her took his breath away. Her hair was in some kind of up-do, a few tendrils coming down to frame her face. The gown she wore was stunning, but her smile was what stopped his heart. She looked like a princess about to go to her first ball. He cleared his throat. "You look amazing."

She peered up at him. "Thanks. I think I'm going to throw up."

Harrison laughed. She never ceased to surprise him. "You'll do fine. It's just Josephine." He held out his arm, and she took it.

"I'm not worried about her. It's the rest of them that scare me."

Harrison opened the front door, and they stepped into the grand foyer. He leaned over. "Just picture them in their underwear."

She snorted and hit his arm. "That's for public speaking."

"Works here, too."

Josephine rushed to them and grabbed Penny's arm. She looked like she had on every piece of jewelry she owned. "Darling, I'm so delighted you're here. You must come meet the Wilsons. They've been dying to meet the young woman who caught Harrison's eye."

He held in a snort. Of course the gossip about them had spread. Penny would be paraded about, shown off like some trinket. They'd cozy up to her tonight, but their tongues would wag long after she'd left. He sighed and trailed along behind them, weaving through the crowd.

The Wilsons were a young couple who lived up the street. They were what his stepmother referred to as 'new rich,' as if a person was less important because their great-grandfather didn't have money. The term left a bad taste in Harrison's mouth.

The Wilsons were chatting with Patrice. As they neared, Patrice turned and plastered on a fake smile. "Well, look who we have here. We were just talking about you."

Patrice pulled an imaginary piece of lint off Harrison's suit jacket, then turned to Penny. "And you." Her smile turned into a sneer. "Aren't you dressed up nice? A bit too formal, maybe?"

Penny's cheeks flushed pink, and Harrison stepped between them. "Mother," he said, his tone a warning. He clenched his fists behind his back so he wouldn't do anything to embarrass himself. Like cram one down her throat.

Josephine either hadn't heard, or ignored the comment. "Penny, this is Liza Wilson and her husband, Frank."

Liza, who was about as tall as most twelve year olds, beamed. "What a pleasure. I've heard so much about you."

Harrison didn't doubt it. Penny took Liza's hand. "So nice to meet you."

As they traded pleasantries, Harrison tugged at his tie. The room had grown too hot. Patrice leaned over to him. "What's the matter? Are you regretting your rash decision to marry a Las Vegas hooker?"

He gritted his teeth and tugged Patrice away from the group. "She's not a prostitute. You have to stop."

Her expression turned contrite. "I'm sorry, dear. You know I just want what's best for you."

"No, you don't. You want what's best for *you*."

Her lips curled up into a smile. "And those are one and the same."

Penny laughed at something Josephine had said, and turned to him. "We'll have to do that."

Uh oh, what had she agreed to? Harrison drew closer to her, leaving his stepmother. "Do what?"

Josephine grabbed his arm. "You'll have to forgive me. I must go welcome more guests." She glided out of the room.

The conversation waned, and everyone stood there, staring at each other. It seemed like a decent time to pull away. "It was nice chatting with you," Harrison said.

When they were out of earshot, he got up the courage to ask. "What did you sign us up for?"

She looked up at him and grinned in a playful manner. "Wouldn't you like to know? What was the Wicked Witch of the West saying to you?"

Harrison shook his head. "It doesn't matter." Why was the room so hot? His gaze connected with hers, which didn't help the heat. He ushered her through the crowd and out onto the terrace. The cool night air washed over him, and he leaned on the rail.

Penny touched his arm, the contact causing his heart to stutter. "Are you okay?"

He wasn't, but he nodded anyway. There weren't words to say what he was feeling. All his life he'd worked for what he had. Wanted to carry on the Williams name. And for what? To go to stupid parties and hang out with these people? It made his life seem so pointless.

The silence stretched between them for a moment, before Penny softly asked, "What did she say?"

"She went too far." He stared out at the lights of the city. "Called you a hooker."

Penny blinked and her eyes filled with tears. Harrison turned toward her and grasped her arms. "I'm sorry, I shouldn't have told you. Don't cry."

She looked down at her shoes. "I don't know what I did to make her hate me."

Her sadness cut through to his heart. "It's not you. She hates giving up control. She wants me under her thumb, like I've always been. I did something without her approval."

"I'm not like these people."

He wiped a tear from her cheek. "Thank goodness."

A laugh bubbled up from her, and Harrison joined in. She smiled at him through her tears. "You always know what to say."

He wrapped his arms around her, pulling her close and tucking her beneath his chin. His chest tightened, and an intense longing to kiss her overwhelmed him. Was he falling for his wife? He pushed the thought from his head. He couldn't afford to think like that.

"Harrison?" she asked, quietly.

He pulled back to look her in the eyes.

"What are we going to do about your stepmother's demands? We can't stay married."

Harrison nodded. "I've contacted my lawyers. They're working on it. Since she changed the stipulations after our marriage started, we might be able to get to the trust fund money."

"Okay."

"Don't worry. We'll get through this." The words felt thick on his tongue. He didn't want to get through this. He wanted to hold her tight and never let go.

Her eyes closed, and she sighed. "I know. It's just—"

"What?"

She peered up at him. "I think it's time to move out."

⁂

Penny bit her lip. Had she said too much? Put her nose where it didn't belong? Harrison's brows pulled together in confusion. "You want to move out?"

"No." Penny laughed. "I think *you* should move out. I mean, it's none of my business and all, but isn't it time to get your own place?"

"Oh." Harrison scratched his chin. "Of course. That makes perfect sense."

"It does?"

He smiled. "Yeah. It's just that…" He turned away from her and grabbed the terrace railing, his knuckles white. "I can't afford to move out."

Penny's mouth fell open. "What do you mean?"

Harrison shook his head, and leaned over. "I don't have the money. Not enough to get a place in L.A. The firm is worth billions, not me. Patrice controls all the money. I only have a few thousand in the bank."

Astonishment washed over her. "Don't you get paid at your job?"

"Yes." He sighed. "At least, I used to. The investment group hasn't been doing so well the past few years. Money's been tight. It was either lay someone off, or stop taking a salary."

Penny swallowed the lump that had grown in her throat. She looked down at the three thousand dollar dress she'd put on his credit card. Oh, no. Panic filled her. "Why did you tell me to buy this dress?"

He shrugged. "It's okay."

"No, it's not! I've just spent an enormous amount on a stupid dress! I probably spent the last of your bank account. What are you going to do?"

Harrison looked out at the city lights and mumbled something inaudible.

Penny leaned closer to him. "What?"

Again, he mumbled something she couldn't hear.

She whacked him on the arm. "Spit it out."

He turned to her. "My stepmother gives me an allowance."

Her first reaction was to laugh, but as soon as the first bit came out and his face fell, she clamped her hand over her mouth. When she was sure no more would come out, she took a breath. "I'm sorry. I didn't mean to laugh. It's just... come on. You're an adult."

His cheeks reddened. "I know. It's technically my money. She's been giving me checks out of the trust fund. She just won't give me the whole thing."

"Because she wants to control you."

He nodded, looking miserable. She had the strangest urge to stroke his cheek and console him, but instead she folded her arms across her chest and tried to ignore the romantic view that stretched before them. "Why does she even want you living there?"

"It's all about having power."

"Ugh. That's so frustrating!"

"Don't worry about it. I'll move out when my attorney forces her to give me access to my trust fund. Should be soon."

Right. Not for two years if The Dragon Lady had anything to say about it. Living with her was making Penny crazy. Who knew how long they'd have to pretend to be married, all the while stepping on eggshells around Patrice? Desperation filled her. "Couldn't we crash at Trent's house? Just for a little while?"

Harrison stared at her like she'd suggested they hit up a bank. "What? Why?"

"It's just difficult. Living with her."

He blinked, then pulled her into his arms. "I'm sorry. You're right. I wasn't thinking."

Really? He would move out just for her? An intense feeling overwhelmed her, and no words would come out.

"I'll look at apartments in the morning. We can rent something. That way I won't need a sizable down payment."

The warm feeling of being wrapped in Harrison's arms enveloped her. The masculine smell of his cologne mixed with his scent made her head spin. She nestled her cheek against his chest, overcome with gratitude for him. "Thank you."

Guilt began to worm its way into her heart, but she shook it off. Harrison needed to get a place of his own. He was thirty, for heaven's sake. It was far past time. She wasn't being selfish. She was helping him stand on his own two feet.

At least that was what she kept telling herself.

CHAPTER 15

Penny's mood had lightened considerably now that Harrison had promised they would start looking at apartments. She pushed all thoughts of Patrice from her mind and started enjoying the party atmosphere. A live band played holiday music while they mingled. Harrison introduced her to quite a few people. Everyone seemed genuinely interested in her.

Miranda, one of Patrice's friends from the dinner party, walked by them. "Harrison." She arched a brow, then glanced at Penny. Her eyes grew wide and she stopped. "Where did you get your gown? It's divine."

Heat crept into Penny's cheeks. "I got it at Abella's."

Miranda nodded in approval. "It's beautiful. I must go there next week. I've been invited to a party at the Mayor's house, and I don't have a *thing* to wear."

Penny pointed to Miranda's red sequined dress. "Why not this? It's so festive."

Disgust filled Miranda's face. "And wear it twice?"

So many things she could say ran through Penny's mind, like 'Oh, the horror!' and 'I don't know what I was thinking. I should be shot.' But she bit her tongue and held in her smart remarks.

Harrison slid his arm around her. "Why do women worry so much about what they wear? If I wore the same suit to two parties, no one would notice."

Penny smiled. "Yeah. Why should I be judged if I wear this dress again? It wasn't cheap, you know. I might have to sleep in it just to get my money's worth."

Miranda turned a deep shade of purple. With her height challenge and round physique, she looked like a grape. She opened her mouth, but no words came out.

Harrison laughed. "Good idea. In fact, I heard the high school's winter dance is tomorrow. We should crash that and give you another chance to wear it."

Laughter bubbled up. "Awesome! Maybe I can find enough parties so I won't have to take this thing off the rest of the month."

Disapproval filled Miranda's face, and she stalked off and disappeared into the crowd.

Harrison introduced Penny to a trio of women in their silver hair stage. He pointed to each of them. "This is Georgette, Daphne, and Mary. We call this group the neighborhood murderers."

The women giggled like school girls. Georgette spoke up. "We all write mystery novels."

Penny grinned. "That's so cool."

A server with one glass of champagne left on his tray weaved his way through the crowd. Penny had watched the dance all evening, guests plucking glasses off the trays as the servers walked by. As he neared, she reached out and grabbed the champagne flute.

She executed the snatch so perfectly, she mentally patted herself on the back. Usually such a klutz, she'd been worried about embarrassing herself. "What kind of mysteries do you write?"

Daphne motioned to Georgette. "She writes cozy, I write crime, and Mary writes historical."

Penny brought her champagne glass to her lips and was about to take a sip when she noticed lipstick on the side. She froze. Now that she looked at it, she could see the glass was half-empty. Had she picked up someone's discarded glass? Why had she done that? Didn't she pay any attention?

Ugh, what was she supposed to do now? Drink it anyway and pretend it was hers? Put it back on the tray? She glanced around for the server, and found that he hadn't gone very far. She could take three steps and put it back on the tray, if she decided now. If she waited too long, he'd be across the room and it would be awkward.

What should she do? He was now four steps away. Five. She needed to hurry. "Excuse me," she blurted. Maybe if she took quick steps she could catch him before it became awkward. Hurrying, she ran after the man with the tray. Unfortunately, right before she got to him she stepped on the hem of her dress and tripped.

Everything happened in slow motion. She grabbed onto the poor server's arm to try to steady herself. All this did was topple his tray which clattered to the floor, bringing everyone's attention to them. Her momentum pushed her into the startled man, shoving him over, which brought them both down, the rest of her champagne dousing him in the face. Her glass slipped from her hand and rolled under a table.

A few startled cries rang out. Penny landed on top of the server, her legs and dress flying up in a very unladylike manner. Heat enveloped her in a full body blush as she frantically climbed off the staff member and pulled down her skirt to cover her neon pink underwear.

"Are you okay, miss?" the server asked as he stood.

Penny glanced around at all the eyes glued to her. Why

did things like this always happen? "I'm fine," she managed to stammer. She turned and ran smack into Patrice, whose lips curled up into a smug smile.

Penny suddenly didn't care about social niceties. All she wanted to do was disappear. She hiked up her dress and ran from the room.

∽

Harrison took off after Penny, his heart in his throat. How embarrassing for her. She ran out the back patio door and down a stone path toward a well-lit garden. He finally caught up to her on a bridge overlooking a small stream. "Are you okay?"

She turned to him, cringing. "Yeah."

"It's okay. We've all had moments like that." He put his hand on her shoulder and electricity zinged up his arm. He removed it. A light breeze carried her floral scent as she gazed out at the garden.

Penny was so different from what he was used to. She didn't care about money. She only cared that people took her seriously. Tripping and falling in front of everyone had to have been devastating for her. His fingers ached to touch her soft skin. He froze. The feelings surging within him were strong. Stronger than he'd felt in years.

But Penny was not his real wife. He couldn't feel this way toward her. He had to get control of himself. He took a deep breath and exhaled slowly.

Penny covered her cheeks with her hands. "I'm such a screw up."

She'd said the words so softly he barely heard them, but they stabbed him in the chest all the same. "Stop. You're not."

She turned to him, her eyes wide. "On my tenth birthday, we were playing pin the tail on the donkey, and somehow I got way off course and ended up backing up into the coffee table."

"That doesn't sound so bad."

"Yeah, except my cake was on the table, and I sat on it. After that, I was known as Frosting Butt at school."

Harrison bit the inside of his cheek to keep from laughing. "That could have happened to anyone."

Her eyebrows pulled together. "I once set up a lemonade stand. Spent all morning making signs, and then setting up the table. Unfortunately it was windy that day and I ended up with lemonade on my lap. You know what that looks like to all the neighborhood kids?"

"That must have been hard for you, but neither one of those is your fault."

"What about the time I was applying for college and mixed up the applications. I sent them to the wrong colleges. My family still laughs about that one."

She looked so distraught, he didn't dare smile. "A simple mistake."

"I once gave a homeless man a twenty dollar bill. Except he wasn't homeless, and I got a thirty minute lecture from an attorney on making assumptions."

Harrison hooked his finger under her chin and forced her to look into his eyes. "You are not a screw up. You are a beautiful woman, with a kind heart. You are intelligent and talented, and anyone would be crazy not to love you." He tucked her under his chin and hugged her close.

~

Penny swallowed. Did he just say he loved her? No. He couldn't have. She listened to his heart beat and tried to suppress the growing feelings inside her. He wasn't saying he loved her. He was only trying to make her feel better.

He was a sweet and caring guy. That was it. She couldn't put anything on him that wasn't there. She needed to put aside all her foolish romantic notions. What had happened with William proved that.

She pulled away from him. "Thank you." She took three more steps away. "I'm fine."

"Are you sure?" Worry filled his face.

"Yep! I'm good." She tried to plaster a smile on her face, but her cheeks felt wooden.

The sound of heels clicking on the stone path rang through the clearing, and Josephine appeared. "Penny. Come here, sweetie." She pulled Penny into an embrace. "Are you okay?"

"I'm fine, Josephine. Really." The more she said it, the more it felt true. She could handle this.

Josephine took her hands in hers. "Don't feel bad, honey. Just about everyone in there has had something embarrassing happen to them." She lowered her voice. "And a couple of them had it splashed all over the papers."

"That would be terrible."

"The best thing to do is march back in there and smile like nothing happened. Tomorrow you'll be old news."

"Wise advice." She could do that. Maybe.

Josephine grinned at her. "Now, a little birdy told me you have a beautiful singing voice. I always have entertainment at my parties. Come sing us a Christmas song and give everyone a new reason to talk about you."

Penny stared at Josephine. Who had said she could sing? Was it…? She glanced at Harrison. He nodded his encouragement. "Go ahead."

Nervousness and excitement shot through her at once. This could be her chance. There were people at this party who could make things happen. She wrung her hands. "Really? You'd let me sing?"

Josephine smiled wide. "I insist."

Could she do it? She kind of liked the idea of slinking in and staying out of sight until it was time to leave. Could she really get up on a stage after showing everyone her underwear?

Indecision plagued her for a moment as she tried to convince herself it didn't matter. No one cared about her fall. She was a performer, and the show must go on. Penny took a deep breath and clenched her fists. "I'll do it."

CHAPTER 16

Penny steeled herself for the curious stares she was sure to receive and followed Josephine through the patio door. Ignoring the gawking, she imagined she was alone, walking through the lavishly decorated home. It was almost like a fairy tale, with the twinkling lights and the bright Christmas bows. If she focused on them, maybe she could do this.

Josephine stepped up onto the stage and took the microphone. The band quickly ended their song. Josephine cleared her throat. "Ladies and gentleman, I have an announcement."

The conversation died down to a hushed level. Penny's mouth dried out, and she tried not to wipe her sweaty hands on the expensive dress.

"We have a special gift for you this evening. We are going to start off the live entertainment with a song sung by a very talented young woman. She recently debuted in Las Vegas, singing in the Whitney Houston tribute show. Please welcome to our stage, Penny Williams!"

Josephine glided off the stage and gave Penny a little one-armed hug. "Just tell the band which song you'll sing."

Penny lifted her skirt a little so she wouldn't trip on the way up to the stage. Her ankles wobbled and she steadied herself. She was not going to mess this up. She could do this. Show them she was more than a klutz with hot pink underwear.

She whispered to the band and stepped up to the microphone. Her stomach rolled and twisted enough to make itself into a pretzel. She took a deep breath and smiled at the sea of faces staring up at her. A nervous giggle escaped. "I guess I'm your entertainment for the night, although my first act was accidental."

A smattering of chuckles made its way through the room, giving her confidence.

"Hopefully this will outshine the first." She glanced back at the band and they started the first strains of O Holy Night.

She didn't miss her intro, and her voice carried over the speakers, clear and steady. Closing her eyes and letting the music take her away, she sang the song that moved her the most during the Christmas season. She imagined she was in a giant cathedral, the sound echoing up to the vaulted ceiling.

As she approached the crescendo, her spirit soared, and she no longer cared what everyone thought of her. Singing took her to another existence. One where she was all she ever hoped to be, and she didn't come up short. Nothing tainted her. She was free.

Her voice quieted as the song ended, and she looked out over the audience. Josephine beamed up at her. Harrison's face was hard to read. Patrice scowled. But the rest of them had awed expressions on their faces. The audience burst into applause.

Josephine was at her side in an instant, and took the microphone. "I think I speak for us all when I say that was phenomenal. You could give Celine Dion a run for her money. Thank you for singing for us. I think we got a real treat tonight."

Being compared to Celine made Penny blush. She stumbled off the stage, her heart beating wildly in her chest.

Harrison pulled her close. "That was amazing." His voice seemed husky.

The rest of the evening went by in a blur. Countless people expressed their awe at her singing talent. She was glad most people had forgotten her embarrassing fall.

When she and Harrison were finally left alone for a moment, she took a deep breath and exhaled.

Harrison tucked her under his arm and whispered, "Are you ready to leave?"

She nodded, grateful once again for his thoughtful nature. They said their goodbyes and Harrison guided her outside. Their car was brought to them and Harrison opened the door for her.

He slid into the driver's seat and turned to her, his expression serious. "You did fantastic tonight."

She bit back a laugh. "Yeah, the whole tripping over myself was great."

A frown crossed his face as he pulled out onto the street. "Why do you always focus on the negative?"

She stared down at her lap. "Sorry. It's habit."

"I've noticed. But so much went well tonight. Your singing…it was…" Harrison stopped talking and Penny glanced up to see him struggling for words. "You moved people."

She blinked, unsure what to say. Was he talking about himself? "Thanks."

"You're special, Penny. Don't you ever forget that."

His words hung in the air and Penny didn't know how to respond. A lump formed in her throat. The car began to seem impossibly small. They pulled into his stepmother's driveway, and she practically leapt out as soon as they stopped.

She had to get away from Harrison. Away from those handsome blue eyes. Away from the way he was making her feel. She ran up to the house, but instead of escaping, she found the door locked. Great. She waited while Harrison got out of the car and made his way up the walk.

"You okay?" His eyebrow raised curiously.

"Yes." She tried to sound bright and cheery. "Sorry. I'm just dying to get out of this dress."

He smiled and stepped closer to unlock the door. "No sleeping in it tonight?"

Arg. Was he flirting with her? Surely he wasn't. But then why was her stomach full of butterflies? And why did she feel this incredible urge to flirt back? She shook her head and entered the house. "Nope. I'm taking this dress off right now."

Penny didn't realize how that sounded until it came out of her mouth. She turned to see Harrison's smile widen. Heat seared her cheeks. "I mean, I'm going to go change. Into something. Comfortable. Yes, that's it. I'm putting on clothes."

He chuckled. "Okay. Go right ahead." He motioned to the grand staircase.

She didn't need a written invitation. She darted up the steps and locked herself in Harrison's bathroom. Oh, dear. Why did she feel this way toward him? No, this wasn't good. She could not fall for him. Not when her head was so confused.

Splashing cold water on her face, she held her breath, trying to calm down. This was all just a mistake. Harrison wasn't flirting. And she wasn't falling for him.

An idea popped into her head as she dried off with a soft towel. She must be on the rebound from William breaking her heart. Of course. That was all. Her heart was latching onto the first male she'd seen after her break up.

She almost giggled as she slipped into her pajamas. A rebound crush. It really was ridiculous when she thought about it. Harrison Williams the Third, heir to a multibillion dollar corporation…and her?

A laugh escaped as she exited the bathroom. No way. Not likely.

Harrison glanced up from his laptop, his body stretched out on the recliner. "What's so funny?" He'd changed out of his suit and was now sporting a white t-shirt and lounge pants.

"Oh, nothing." She imagined what it would be like to marry him, and then stopped short. She had married him. In a Las Vegas quickie church! With her father in his purple polyester suit. A snicker escaped and she clamped her lips together.

He shot her a look and it reminded her of the day she met him, standing at the altar, and how she'd thought he was just grumpy because he didn't like crowds. The absurdity of the situation got to her and she laughed out loud.

Harrison moved the laptop to the end table. "Come on. Now you have to tell me."

She sat down on the bed and tried to calm her giggles, but the image of him staring distastefully at her orange Pacer made her laughter uncontrollable. Tears blurred her vision and she wiped at her eyes, her sides hurting.

"Is it something I did?"

His words made her laugh even more, and she rolled over on the bed. Harrison must have gotten frustrated with her because the springs squeaked as he sat next to her. "What?"

She knew she had to say something, so between gulps of air she managed to say, "We're married!"

A scowl crossed his face. "Yeah. I know." When her giggles

didn't subside, his eyebrows knit together. "You think that's funny?"

She swallowed another laugh and pointed at him. "You..." A fit of giggles came out. "You thought...I...was a rich girl!"

That got him, and Harrison let out a belly laugh. "You're right, that is funny."

"Your face...when you found out. It was...so hilarious!" She hiccupped and both of them dissolved into laughter.

Penny was out of breath when they finally settled down. She and Harrison were both on their backs, staring up at the ceiling. When her breathing slowed, she chanced a glance at him. He looked contemplative. "What are you thinking?"

The silence weighed heavy on her while she waited for him to answer. He took a breath. "I can't tell you."

She whacked him on the arm. "Why not?"

"Because I shouldn't be thinking it." He stood and left the room, leaving Penny to stare after him in confusion.

CHAPTER 17

Harrison glanced around the small apartment's living room / dining room / mini kitchen and tried not to frown. It was newly renovated, which was nice, but the size…well, he and Penny would be quite cozy. "How much a month?"

"Eleven hundred." The realtor rubbed her hands together. "A real bargain, considering the location, and it includes parking." She grinned at him and for some reason he imagined a shark's head coming out of her tailored pant suit.

He glanced at Penny and lowered his voice. "What do you think?"

She chewed her bottom lip. "That seems like a lot." Her gaze traveled over the room. "Maybe we shouldn't move out."

His heart sank. She didn't like it. Of course not. Compared to his stepmother's mansion, this was more appropriate for a hamster. "I know it's not much…"

"Oh, that's not it." She shook her head and grabbed his hand. "It's just, I don't know if we can afford it. Without… you know."

That was sweet. She didn't want to say, 'your allowance'

in front of the realtor. How had he allowed that situation to materialize anyway? He should have insisted on the firm paying him a salary and stayed away from Patrice's manipulations. "Don't worry. I'll take care of the finances. Do you like the apartment?"

A small smile crept over her face. "It's perfect."

He turned to the realtor. "We'll take it."

~

Penny followed Harrison out to the car and climbed in. She couldn't wipe the smile off her face. They were moving out! Not right away. They couldn't occupy the apartment until the first of January, but Harrison had signed a lease. Fake married life was going to be much more awesome away from Ms. Frosty Cold Pants.

She didn't care about the pool or any of the other fancy stuff. She'd lived her whole life without all that. Not important. Just being with Harrison was enough.

Wait.

Penny shook her head. What was she thinking? She gripped the leather seat and closed her eyes. She had to stop. Harrison was working with his lawyers right now to get his trust fund, and she could be off finding her own place soon. Thinking about that future somehow didn't seem as appealing to her. She turned up the radio and tried not to dwell on the depressing fact that she had no job and no home.

Harrison parked the car in his stepmother's driveway, and they entered the house. "We'd better start packing. Our flight is in the morning."

Excitement shot through her. Christmas with her family. Trimming the tree and driving around to look at the lights. Singing carols with her sister. Her heart warmed until she realized she'd have to spend the whole time calling Harrison 'William' and pretending she hadn't made the biggest blunder of her life.

A sinking feeling swept over her.

Harrison raised an eyebrow. "I thought you were excited to go see your family."

Penny drew in a deep breath. "I am. It's just…" She waved a hand between them. "All this."

Harrison's expression turned unreadable, and he slowly nodded. "I see."

"But like you said, we'd better start packing." She headed for the stairs, but Harrison didn't move. What was up with him? She had no idea, so she climbed the stairs anyway.

As she threw things together, Harrison walked in and sat on the bed. "Patrice has agreed to celebrate Christmas a little early since we're going to your parents' house. We'll be exchanging gifts tonight."

Penny froze. What? Gifts? She hadn't gone shopping. She had no money. What would she get her? The look on her face must have given away her thoughts because Harrison said, "Don't worry. I bought her tickets to a charity gala event. They'll be from both of us."

"Oh good." Penny let out a breath she'd been holding. "I suddenly panicked."

He laughed. "I could tell. Don't stress. I got something for Trent and Candy too."

As she folded a sweater, she wondered what else they did here for Christmas celebration. She couldn't see Patrice in the kitchen making cookies, and the decorations were most likely put up by the staff. "What other traditions do you have?"

He shrugged. "We always eat shrimp cocktail, which I'm sure Annabel will serve. Besides that and the gift exchange, we don't do much else."

"Even when you were a kid?"

"Things were a little more festive when I was a kid. We'd sing carols on Christmas Eve, and take goodies to the neighbors. And we'd get Santa gifts on Christmas morning. But after Mom died and my father re-married, we stopped doing all that. Patrice isn't into music, baking's beneath her, and she doesn't like anyone else getting credit for the gift giving, I guess." He smiled, but his eyes remained cold. "Dad always seemed to be at work."

Penny sat on the bed next to him and put her hand on his. "I'm sorry."

"No need to feel sorry for me." He motioned around the room. "I grew up here. Christmas meant more gifts than we could count."

A wave of sadness washed over her. "But you missed the very best parts of it."

He reached out and brushed her hair from her face, then trailed the back of his finger down her cheek to her jaw. "I guess you'll have to show me how it's supposed to be done."

His touch was making her insides turn to Jell-O, so she grabbed his hand and pushed it away. "Deal."

~

Patrice sat in the wingback chair at the head of the room, her back straight and her ankles crossed. Harrison rolled his eyes. Did she ever get tired of her pious attitude? He squeezed Penny's hand to let her know that he'd protect her if necessary.

Trent and Candy sat on the couch near the fireplace across from him and Penny on the loveseat. The staff had handed out the gifts and were now standing against the wall as was the custom.

The air in the room smelled stale and Harrison tugged

uncomfortably on his tie. In the past it hadn't seemed odd that they dressed up for their Christmas celebration, but tonight it felt out of place. He wished he could relax in a T-shirt and jeans.

Patrice stood and handed each of the staff an envelope. Their Christmas bonuses. Annabel opened hers first. "Thank you, ma'am." She did a little curtsy.

Antonio's hands shook as he slid his finger under the flap. The relief on his face at seeing the check made Harrison wonder. Were they not paying him enough for his services? Antonio wiped a hand over his sweaty brow and swallowed, making the eagle tattoo on his neck move. "Thank you, ma'am." Patrice and Antonio exchanged a glance.

Everyone watched as the rest of them opened their checks and uttered their thanks to Patrice. Then she dismissed them with a curt wave of her hand.

Penny looked like she wanted to say something, but held it in.

Trent stretched his arm around Candy and put his feet up on the coffee table. "Are we going to open our presents now or just stare at each other?"

A glare crossed Patrice's face, but she smoothed out her features. "It's time. Trent, why don't you go first?"

"Okay. This one is to me and Candy from Harrison and Penny." He picked up a package and tore open the paper. "Ah, a personalized wine box." He held it up for everyone to see. "Thanks, Bro."

"It does have a little something inside," Harrison said.

Trent opened the box and whistled. "Moet and Chandon Dom Perignon Oenotheque Rose. 1990." He shot Harrison a grin. "Wow."

"I thought you two might enjoy that."

Candy grinned and took it from Trent. "You know I like bringing out the good stuff when we have company."

Trent pulled it back from her. "I think this one we'll keep."

Harrison chuckled to himself.

Penny poked him in the side. "How much did that cost?" she whispered.

"Twelve hundred."

Penny's eyes grew wide and her mouth dropped. "Are you crazy?"

"I bought it before we decided to..." He let his voice trail off when he realized everyone was listening to them. "Never mind. We'll discuss it later."

Patrice's lips pinched together in a tight line, and she motioned for Harrison to open something next. He picked up the small gift from his stepmother. "From you."

He slipped his finger under the paper and loosened the tape.

Penny nudged him. "You're acting like you're going to reuse that paper. Just rip it."

Knowing that the slow unwrap bugged her made him want to do it all the more. He grinned and took his time with the tape on the other side.

Penny scoffed but didn't say anything else.

When he'd gotten the paper off, he opened the jewelry box. A Rolex. "Thank you, Mother." He'd put it in his drawer with the others.

Patrice nodded and shifted in her seat. "Penny, why don't you open your gift next?" The way she said it—and the smug look that took over her face—made Harrison's guard go up. What had Patrice gotten her?

Penny picked up the present and ripped off the paper. She held up plastic snowman ornament. "It's adorable!" Either she was a fabulous actress, or she didn't realize the cheap gift was an insult. Penny examined it, smiling. "It even has the year on it. Thank you, Patrice."

The smug expression slowly faded into a frown. "You're welcome, dear."

They opened the rest of the presents, wished each other a Merry Christmas, and Harrison steered Penny out of the room without any other incidents. He breathed a sigh of relief when he closed their bedroom door.

Penny held up the earrings that Trent and Candy had given her. "These are so pretty. They shine just like real diamonds."

He smiled in amusement while loosening his tie. "They *are* real diamonds."

She whacked him on the arm. "Get out."

"I assure you, they are."

Penny gaped at him. "I've never owned diamonds before."

A rush of guilt pressed down on his chest as he looked at the cheap metal still on her finger. Even though their marriage wasn't real, he should have made sure her ring was. This was something he needed to rectify as soon as possible.

He wiped a hand over his face. If his deficient bank account weren't stopping him. How had he let the situation with Patrice grow so out of control? He stepped out onto the balcony and let the cool breeze wash over him. He couldn't take money from the firm. Not when it would mean layoffs. He had to get access to his trust fund.

Outside, the clicking of heels on the stone walkway below echoed up to the balcony. He leaned over the railing. What was Patrice doing out by the garage this time of night? He watched as she disappeared into the shadows.

CHAPTER 18

Nerves shot through Penny as she boarded the plane and followed Harrison up the aisle. "We'll be trimming the tree tonight. And after that we always go driving around to look at all the Christmas lights, then we go back home and have eggnog." The more she talked about it, the more excited she got.

Harrison looked over his shoulder, a grin on his face. "You're like a little kid."

"It's Christmas! And I wasn't able to make it back home last year. I missed out on everything." She pushed thoughts of last year away. She'd been on stage then, pursuing a dead-end singing career. Couldn't get the time off, and ended up eating cold Chinese food alone in her apartment, texting William.

No. She couldn't think of all the time wasted on that sleazebag. If she allowed herself to think of him, she'd be mad all through the holiday festivities. Better to forget him altogether and enjoy the time with her family.

Harrison squeezed into his seat, looking like he'd never flown coach before. She was proud of him for giving up some comfort to save money. He shoved his bag under the seat in front of him and turned to her. "Is your sister going to be there?"

"Yes, Kimmy's on break from school. And Clay's a senior, so he's still at home." It hit her that this might be the last Christmas with all of them together for a while, with Kimmy and Clay both graduating and running off to who knew where.

"Are you close?"

Penny took a deep breath. They'd been close growing up, but time and space had distanced them. She should have been better about calling them. She fiddled with a strap on her bag. "I guess I've allowed things to get between us. But we're family. I love them, even though sometimes I want to punch them in the throat."

Harrison's deep chuckle washed over her and she peeked at him. He looked like she'd picked him out of a catalogue. His chiseled features and smooth skin could rival any Greek god. She turned her gaze away. She'd better keep to the task at hand.

"Anything I should know before spending time with your family? What did you tell them about William?"

Yeah. William. Her nerves came back a hundred fold. She'd have to spend Christmas calling him William. Pretending he was William. Thinking about William. Gah. William would haunt her all week. And what if she messed up, like she always did?

Harrison pried her hand off the chair rail and warmed it between his hands. "Hey, calm down. Everything is going to be fine. They've never met William, right? So if we make a mistake, we can just say communication got screwed up while we chatted online."

She drew in a breath. "You're right. It will work out. I didn't tell my family much about William anyway. I didn't want them to laugh at me for falling for someone I'd never met."

The words almost choked in her throat. If her family only knew the whole story, they'd never stop laughing. Harrison squeezed her hand and she blinked back the tears threatening to spill.

"I'm not going to let them laugh at you." He spoke the words so quietly she almost didn't hear them.

Warmth spread through her. How did he do that? He always knew what to say to make her feel better. "Thanks."

The flight was uneventful, which gave Penny ample time to stew about Harrison pretending to be William. When they landed in Des Moines she was a bundle of nerves.

As soon as she saw her mother, her throat tightened. How would she keep up this charade? Why had she thought this was a good idea?

Her mother rushed to her and enveloped her in a warm hug. "Hi, you two. So nice to see you. How was your flight?" She held Penny at arm's length and studied her. "Something's wrong. I can always tell when something is bothering you. Are you okay?" A frown crossed her mother's face.

Dang. Lying was going to be hard. "I'm fine, Mom."

"You're not ill, are you? You look a little pale. Wait, are you pregnant?" A hopeful smile lit up her face.

"No, Ma! Stop." Heat seared Penny's cheeks. "I think I'm just hungry. We left so early I wasn't up to breakfast and all we had on the plane were some pretzels." At least part of that was true.

Her mother pulled Harrison into a quick hug.

"Nice to see you again, Mrs. Ackerman."

"Call me Marci, dear. Mrs. Ackerman was my mother-in-law, and she was as cold as they come."

Harrison laughed. "Marci it is."

Her mother smiled. "Well, we need to get you two home. I'll whip up some lunch."

◈

Harrison plopped the suitcases down and took in the small bedroom. The walls were painted light purple, and half the ceiling slanted, cutting down the space where he'd be able to stand upright. The bedspread had a floral print, and a white dresser with a mirror took up the wall beside the tiny closet. Photos covered almost the entire mirror, with just enough space in the middle to see his own reflection.

Before he had time to examine the photos, Penny came in. "Oh, they've left my room exactly the same." She smiled and the room felt brighter. Her hair swayed as she glanced around. "Sorry it's so cramped in here." She worried her lip.

"It's fine, really. Cozy." He rubbed the back of his neck. "I'm just worried about the uh…there's no chair…"

Penny pulled open her closet door and brought out a sleeping bag and a large body pillow. "It's okay. I'll sleep on the floor. I used to do it all the time when my cousins came to visit."

Harrison couldn't let her do that. "I can take the floor." Before she could protest he grabbed her hand. "Let's go help your mother."

When they got to the kitchen, Marci had everything already out and was putting mayonnaise on the bread. It was obvious Penny got her height from her father. Penny's mother could barely reach the top cupboards. "Are you two all settled in? How was your honeymoon? I was going to call but I wanted to give you some privacy."

Penny's face blanched, so Harrison stepped in. "The

honeymoon was wonderful, wasn't it, sweetheart? We lounged on the beach and soaked up the sun."

Alarm filled Penny's eyes. Marci raised an eyebrow while reaching for another piece of bread. "The beach? I thought you were honeymooning in Alaska."

Alaska? What? Now what was he supposed to do? Penny swallowed and tugged at her sweater. "William had mentioned Alaska, but at the last minute we decided somewhere warm would be better, right honey?"

He nodded. "Right. We went to Hawaii instead."

A high-pitched squeal came from the doorway and Harrison turned to see Kim, who looked like a cookie cutter version of Penny except with very short hair that stood up on end. "You got to go to Hawaii? You lucky duck."

Penny smiled and hugged her sister. "I didn't know you were home yet. I love your haircut! So cute!"

"Just got here, and thanks."

Marci gave Kim a one armed hug while holding a butter knife with the other. "How were the roads?"

"A little icy near Lincoln, but the interstate was clear."

The kitchen really wasn't big enough for all of them, but no one seemed to care. Kim picked up a sandwich and Marci slapped at her hand. "Stop that, these are for the newlyweds."

Kim took a large bite and scooted out of the way so Marci couldn't catch her. Then with her mouth full, said, "You snooze you lose."

Marci scowled at her retreating daughter. "Kimmy!"

Penny laughed. "Not a problem. I'll make another one." She picked up the bread and a slice of ham.

Marci shook her head, and then sighed. "I think we're all still adjusting to the idea of you being married. I mean, when I first found out, I was quite worried. The Internet is full of people pretending to be something they're not. But now that

I've met you, William…" A warm smile filled her face. "I can see you are something special."

A cold lump of guilt weighed heavily in his stomach. No way to go back now. He had to keep up the charade. "Thank you, Marci. And I can see why Penny is the delightful person I fell in love with. She comes from a wonderful family."

Marci patted him on the arm and kissed his cheek. "You're a dear."

After they'd eaten lunch, Harrison stood and took the plates. "I can put them in the dishwasher."

"A man who does the dishes?" Kim whacked Penny on the arm. "No wonder you fell in love."

A smile took over Penny's face. "He cooks, too."

Marci stood and picked up the glasses. "What do you like to cook?"

"All kinds of things. Actually, ever since Penny told me you usually have eggnog after you look at Christmas lights, I've been wondering if you'd let me try my hand at making some. I've always wanted to."

"Only if it's non-alcoholic," Marci said. "Arthur's been sober ten years, and we don't allow any of that in the house."

"Sure, I can make it without the rum."

"Then we'll happily be your guinea pigs." Marci placed her last glass in the dishwasher then added the soap and turned it on. "The sauce pans are in here, and the spices up there. Help yourself."

~

While Harrison busied himself in the kitchen, Penny found herself the focus of curious stares from her sister. Finally, she turned to her and blurted, "What?"

Kimmy shifted in the worn living room chair her parents

had ever since she could remember. "I don't know. You just seem to be happier. I think William's good for you."

Penny studied her sister. "What do you mean?"

"I don't know." Kimmy shrugged. "I was just watching you while we were eating. He'd touch your arm and you'd blush. You'd say something and he'd smile and look at you like he couldn't get enough of you. I think you make a good couple."

Well, fooling Kimmy had been easier than she'd thought. If she could get over the whole William breaking her heart thing, maybe she could enjoy this Christmas. "Yeah, I think so, too. What about you? Are you seeing anyone?"

A looked crossed Kimmy's face that told it all. Penny slapped her knee. "You are! Tell me all about him."

Kimmy scooted closer and lowered her voice. "If I tell you, you are sworn to secrecy."

"Of course." Guilt surged in Penny for prying secrets out of her sister when she was keeping a whopper herself.

"Last summer I ran into Rob Curtis at the five and dime. He and I sort of hit it off."

Penny's mouth dropped open. "Rob Curtis? The biker Rob Curtis?"

Kimmy waved her hand. "Shh! Keep your voice down. If mom found out, I'd be in so much trouble."

"What are you doing with him, Kimmy?" Penny whisper-shouted. "I thought you were smarter than that."

"He's actually really nice. You shouldn't judge until you've gotten to know someone."

Her mother walked in and Penny jerked back from Kimmy. "I know, I can't wait to make candy cane cookies either."

It was a lame attempt, but her mother didn't seem to notice. "They've always been your favorite."

Harrison entered the room and sat beside Penny on the loveseat, putting his arm around her. "What's your favorite?"

His smell enveloped Penny and she found it hard to think. What was the name of his cologne, Male Yumminess in a Bottle? She gave in and snuggled up to him. "Candy cane cookies."

Kimmy grinned and poked her. "You're doing it again."

"Doing what?"

"You know, acting like a happily in-love sister."

Ha. If only Kimmy could sit beside him and smell this. Then she'd understand. Best to keep up the act, though. "That's because I am." She leaned over and gave Harrison a kiss.

CHAPTER 19

Penny should have thought about it more before she kissed Harrison. The idea was to pretend she was happily in love, but as soon as her lips touched his, she melted in his arms and the pretend part flew out the window. His warm lips were soft and inviting, and she felt like she'd taken a bite of a forbidden dessert, only to want a hundred more. She pulled away and forced herself to sit rigidly beside him, avoiding as much contact as possible.

She couldn't fall in love with Harrison. He was…dang he was perfect. He always said the right thing. He was a gentleman who treated her with respect. He knew how to make her laugh. And he was out of her reach.

Harrison deserved a woman raised with poise and grace. Someone who could live in his world, and who Patrice didn't hate. Penny had been born in Iowa, in a hick town with two stoplights. She was the person who fell over her own feet and made embarrassing messes at parties. She could never fit into Harrison's world.

"What do you think, Penny?" Her mother stared at her, waiting for her to respond.

Her cheeks heated. "Sorry, I wasn't listening."

Harrison leaned toward her. "Your mother thinks we should get some family photos taken."

A hole opened up in her chest. Photos. So years from now she could remember what a colossal mistake she'd made in marrying the wrong guy, and how she'd actually fallen for him, and then how he'd left once the money came. Yeah. Great idea. "Sure." She tried to make her voice sound chipper.

Her mother smiled. "I'll call and make arrangements."

Penny sank down in the chair. Great.

The door opened and Clay plopped his backpack on an empty chair. "Hey, Sis." He gave a polite nod to Harrison then went into the kitchen. "Mmm. What's that smell, and can I have some?"

"William made us homemade eggnog." Her mother trailed after him. "It's chilling in the fridge, but don't you touch it. It's for tonight."

Harrison nudged her. "You okay?"

She plastered on a smile. "Yeah. Just tired I guess."

He must have bought it, because he nodded. "The flight was early. I think I'll sleep well tonight."

Kimmy giggled. "Sure you will." She winked, and heat assaulted Penny's cheeks once more.

"Stop it." Penny whacked her sister with the back of her hand.

"Mom should have gotten you a bigger bed." Kimmy wiggled her eyebrows. "But maybe you two don't mind, being newlyweds and all."

"Kimmy!" Penny could tell her whole body was blushing.

Harrison chuckled beside her and snuggled up close, his arm around her. "You're cute when you're embarrassed." His warm breath caressed her cheek, and even that smelled good. She needed to get away from him, and fast.

Penny stood. "Let's start moving furniture around to make room for the tree."

After they got the living room ready, Penny showed Harrison where the Christmas decorations were, and they brought up several boxes from the basement. It was a good distraction. By the time her father came home, the tree was almost put together, and Kimmy had the lights strung out on the floor.

Her father gave her a big hug, and clapped Harrison on the back. "William, nice to see you again."

"Same to you, Arthur." Harrison looked a little uncomfortable, and Penny wasn't sure if he was intimidated by her father, or if he was feeling guilty about the deception.

"How was work today, Daddy?" Penny couldn't stop calling him Daddy. Her father always made her feel like a little girl.

"It was fine, sweetheart. So good to have you back home." He eyed Harrison as he loosened his tie. "He been treating you well?"

"Of course, Dad." Man, not another blush. She might as well paint herself red and go sit with the candy canes.

Harrison stepped forward. "Penny tells me you're a manager at a meat packing plant. That sounds like an interesting job."

Her dad shook his head. "It's not." He laughed. "But it pays the bills. By the way, Penny was evasive when I asked her what you did for a living."

A deer-in-the-headlights look came onto Harrison's face and he hesitated for a second, glancing at Penny. She hadn't told them anything, since William had never answered her questions about work, so she shrugged.

"I work for an investment company."

"Which one?" Her dad raised an eyebrow.

"Harrison Williams Investment Group."

Seemingly impressed, her dad nodded. "That's a large firm. What do you do there?"

Aw, crud. Of course he'd ask. And Harrison couldn't tell the truth, that he was the CEO. Penny took her dad's arm and tugged him toward the kitchen. "Enough boring stuff. Come see what William made for us tonight."

Penny successfully dodged her father's questions about Harrison all evening as they trimmed the tree and stuffed themselves on Chinese take-out. Then they all piled in the minivan and took to the streets to look at the amazing displays that some of the townsfolk put up this time of year.

It was quite nostalgic driving past old Henry McDermott's house, decked out with the moving Santa display he put up every Christmas. And Mrs. Schmidt's front yard, where she created a candy cane lane you could walk through. The best one was always the Hatchett farm, out by the railroad tracks. They bought a new item each year and kept expanding. They'd won the Best of State award for their display.

Harrison grabbed her hand when they turned around to go back home, and Penny wished she could take it back without it looking weird to her sister. She'd have to talk to Harrison later. This pretending was fine, but the physical contact was killing her. She'd make a new rule. No kissing, handholding, or anything else that made her stomach turn inside out.

When they got back home, her mother brought out the special glasses with the holly leaves on them, and they poured Harrison's eggnog.

Kimmy raised her glass. "To William. For making my sister so happy."

Everyone toasted, and Harrison's ears grew pink. Penny turned away and ignored how cute he looked. In fact, she tried to ignore him all night, but it was impossible when he was constantly beside her, rubbing her back, or whispering in her ear.

By the time they went upstairs for bed, Penny was about ready to scream at him. They entered her childhood room and she shut the door and then turned to face him. "Okay, that's enough."

Harrison blinked. "What did I do?"

"I can't take any more of this." She ran her hands through her hair and had to restrain herself from tugging chunks of it out. "We need to set some rules."

His eyebrows knit together. "What's wrong?"

She ignored him and kept going. "One: No kissing."

"Hey, wait a minute, you kissed me." He put his hands up in a surrender position.

She glared at him, but continued. "Two: No handholding."

"What—"

"Just let me finish!" Frustration welled in her. It wasn't his fault, really. She knew she was acting like a crazy person, but she couldn't stop herself. "Three: No rubbing my back."

Harrison closed his mouth that had been hanging open after she'd interrupted him. He put his hands behind his back and cocked his head at her.

"Four: No more cologne." She looked at him to see if he would object, but he just stood there, staring at her. "Five: No more whispering in my ear." She folded her arms across her chest, trying to think of anything else that was bugging her. Nothing else came to mind, so she raised her chin. "Think you can handle that?"

Harrison frowned. "So, basically you want me to stop acting like we're a married couple."

Glad that he understood, Penny nodded. "Yes."

"I'm sorry I've been bothering you, but is that wise?"

She didn't care if it was wise or not. She couldn't take any more of Harrison's touch. "No one suspects a thing. It'll be fine."

His shoulders drooped and he looked tired. "Okay. If that's what you want."

"Yes, that's what I want."

A moment of silence filled the room before he spoke again. "Can I ask you one thing?"

"Yes."

"What does my cologne have to do with it?"

She didn't want to tell him the truth, so she lied. "I just don't like it."

"All right."

He looked dejected, like she'd told him to quit annoying her or something, but she couldn't explain to him what she was feeling. She couldn't even explain it to herself. She just knew that if he kept touching her she'd go insane. "Good. Glad that's settled. I'll get my pajamas on in the bathroom, and you can change in here."

By the time she got back, Harrison was curled up on the floor, asleep. She climbed into bed and turned out the lamp. Exhaustion seeped from her bones, but no matter how she would lie, she couldn't get to sleep.

"Penny?"

His deep voice startled her and she peered down at him. "What?"

"I'm sorry I made you uncomfortable. That was not my intention."

And there was Mr. Gentleman again, making her feel even worse for blowing up at him. "I know." When he didn't say anything else, she added, "Thanks, Harrison."

CHAPTER 20

Harrison awoke with sore muscles from sleeping on the floor and a sour taste in his mouth. Penny wasn't anywhere in sight, so he grabbed his clothes and went into the bathroom. If he didn't get rid of his grumpy demeanor, he'd end up snapping at everyone. After he showered and dressed, he wandered downstairs to the kitchen. Penny and her mother were deep in discussion when he entered.

Penny turned to him and offered a little smile. She looked amazing. His heart sank in his chest. She was the best thing that ever happened to him, and last night she'd made it clear she didn't want him even touching her.

He swallowed and his throat felt like sandpaper. How was he going to get through the next few days? He needed to call his attorney and see how things were going with the trust fund. The sooner he could get out of this situation and away from Penny, the better. He plastered on a smile to mask his true feelings. "What's up?"

"I was just telling Mom how good your omelets are. And I was wondering…" Penny let the sentence hang.

"Sure, I'll make breakfast."

"Thanks." Penny opened the fridge and pulled out a carton of eggs. "I'll help. What do you need?"

He listed off his favorite ingredients and went in search of a pan. "Why don't you sit and rest for a minute, Marci? We've got this."

An appreciative smile took over her face. "Thank you, William. How nice of you two."

Harrison was glad for the distraction. He found cooking so enjoyable that he was able to zone out and ignore the hole that had opened up in his chest. When he and Penny had finished, they sat down at the small table in the dining room and invited Kimmy and Marci to join them.

Marci took a bite. "This is delicious. How do you get your eggs so fluffy?"

"You beat the egg whites first, and then fold in the beaten yolks," Harrison said.

"Brilliant. You'll have to teach me all of your kitchen tricks." Marci gave Harrison a warm smile.

"I keep telling him he needs to quit his miserable job and open up a restaurant," Penny mumbled as she picked up her glass of water.

Harrison gave Penny a 'what-are-you-doing' look, and she blushed and looked away.

Marci's smile turned stale. "You don't like your job?"

Great. How was he supposed to dance around that subject? "It's fine. I don't hate it."

Penny snorted. "Yes you do. You'd be much happier if you could cook for a living." She tossed a pointed look at Harrison, which he ignored.

Marci fiddled with her fork. "Owning your own business is risky, especially something as unstable as a restaurant. It won't bring in steady income."

"He didn't say he was going to quit his job." Kimmy scoffed and took another bite of her breakfast.

Unable to think of anything else to say, Harrison decided to change the subject. "What's on the schedule for today?"

"The gingerbread house contest is tonight at the community hall," Marci said. "I thought you three might like to enter something."

"Penny told me about that. I guess some people get really into it." He remembered Penny's face as she talked about the different houses and how big and intricate they got. "I'd love to take a stab at it."

"Awesome," Kimmy said. "Maybe this year we'll win."

Harrison smiled but Penny avoided his gaze.

Marci studied them. "Everything okay between you guys?"

Penny's cheeks turned pink. "We're fine, Mom."

Sure, fine. If Marci could see the strain between them now, he couldn't imagine how they'd get through the next few days.

Marci's eyes narrowed. "You know you can't lie to me."

Kimmy set her fork down with a clank. "Ma, let them be."

Penny stared at her plate and Marci leaned back in her chair. "I'm sorry. You're right. I shouldn't stick my nose where it doesn't belong. It just feels like you guys had a fight or something."

Penny reached out and covered Harrison's hand with her own. "Nothing's going on. We're fine." She removed her hand quickly and tucked it into her lap.

"Have you two seen *Fireproof*?"

"Ma!" Kimmy stood and picked up her plate. "Give it a rest."

Harrison stood as well and helped Kimmy clear the table. It was best to get out of that conversation. His phone chimed in his pocket, and he set down the plates on the kitchen counter. The display told him it was his attorney.

Finally. He swiped the screen and held it to his ear. "Michael. What's up?"

The line crackled. "Harrison. I have good news and bad news. Which do you want first?"

He glanced at Kimmy, who was doing a bad job of pretending not to listen. He walked down the hallway to the bathroom and closed the door. "Tell me everything."

"The good news is your stepmother has relinquished control of your trust fund."

Harrison's heart hammered in his chest. That was good news, right? He could pay Penny and get out of this situation. This was what he'd been hoping for, so why did his stomach feel like a cold ball of lead? "That's great. What's the bad?"

"The bad news is there's only twenty five thousand dollars in there."

～

Penny sighed. There was no way they would win the contest. The walls to their gingerbread mansion were sagging, the columns she'd tried to stabilize leaned to the right, and the roof looked like it would slide off at any minute. At least they'd had fun putting it together. Well, she and Kimmy. Harrison had been distracted. When she pulled him aside and tried to talk about it, he brushed her off.

Harrison held the door open and Kimmy entered the community hall carrying their creation. Clay had stayed home, being the typical teen who was too embarrassed to be seen in public with the family. Penny followed Kimmy. Her mom and dad were already inside looking at the entries.

After they got their number and set up their display, they

started down one side of the hall. Harrison had taken her at her word. He hadn't held her hand or done any of the other things that drove her nuts. The problem was she missed it.

Stupid. That's what she was. Why couldn't she make up her mind? Did she want Harrison to leave her alone, or not? Her heart yearned for the closeness they'd come to share, but her head told her he was leaving soon and she needed to steel her heart before it broke in two.

Kimmy grabbed her arm and practically yanked it out of its socket. "Shh, don't say anything, but Rob just entered the hall."

Rob? Penny turned to look, and sure enough, Rob Curtis stood across the room. He wore a leather jacket and had a shaved head and metal piercings in his ears. When his gaze met Kimmy's, he nodded and stuffed his fists in his jacket pockets.

Why was she involved with this loser? Penny wanted to be supportive, but she knew Rob was no good. He'd gotten into some trouble in high school and spent the rest of his senior year in a juvenile detention center. She wasn't sure what he'd done, but she suspected it involved drugs.

Kimmy grinned like a cat with a mouse-tail hanging out of her mouth. "Isn't he handsome?"

Oh, heavens. She had it bad. Penny sighed and shook her head. "Kimmy, do you think—"

"Hey," Kimmy interrupted. "Cover for me, okay?" She patted Penny on the back and disappeared into the crowd. A moment later she emerged by Rob's side. They kissed then ducked out of the building.

"She loves him, doesn't she?" Harrison's deep voice startled her.

Penny whipped around to face him. He had a sad sort of smile on his face, and his eyes held something she couldn't pin down. "Yeah, I think so."

"You don't like him."

She scoffed and motioned over her shoulder. "Did you see him?"

He shrugged one shoulder, staring into her eyes. "I did."

"He's no good for Kimmy."

"Patrice thinks you're no good for me."

"That's different." Penny turned and started walking away, but Harrison stepped in front of her, blocking her. He put his hands on her shoulders.

"Is it? Do you love your sister?"

Penny yanked her shoulders away from Harrison's grasp. "Of course I do."

"Then you've got to let her make her own decisions. She's an adult. If you try to break them up, you'll just hurt your relationship with your sister."

Penny blinked and stared at a gingerbread replica of the leaning tower of Pisa. He was right. She didn't want to admit it, but Harrison made sense. "But he's a criminal."

"What did he do?"

"I don't know. He got in trouble in high school."

Harrison folded his arms across his chest. "That was a long time ago. You've got to trust your sister."

She blew out a frustrated breath. "You're right. I just don't trust *him*."

"Maybe you need to get to know him."

"I can't. Kimmy wants to keep him a secret from our parents. Does that sound like a healthy relationship to you?"

Harrison sighed and ran his fingers through his hair. "Maybe not. But it's not up to you, is it?"

Man, he looked handsome, with his hair slightly disheveled and his five o-clock shadow. She had to look away. "No. It's not."

He placed his hand on her back and she stiffened. He

removed it. "Come on. Let's go look at the rest of the displays. We can talk about your sister later."

Penny nodded, stuffed her conflicted feelings deep down inside, and followed Harrison along the rows of gingerbread houses.

CHAPTER 21

Harrison entered the jewelry store and rubbed the stubble forming on his face. They'd spent the morning baking goodies, and after lunch he'd managed to convince Penny they needed to go shopping for a few last minute Christmas gifts. They'd had a nice afternoon picking out things for Penny's family.

He'd told Penny he needed a quick break and had left her browsing some role-playing games at the geek store. Now here he was, trying to decide if buying her a real ring was a good idea or not.

What he wanted to do was get the perfect ring, and then when they were alone together under a moonlit sky, get down on one knee and profess his love for her. What he feared he'd do would be carry around the ring in his pocket until he lost his nerve and let the woman of his dreams go.

"Can I help you?" A man behind the counter placed his hands on the glass case containing wedding rings. "Anything you'd like to look at?"

Harrison swallowed. This was a bad idea. He didn't even

have enough money to give Penny what he'd promised her. And she'd been clear. No kissing. No touching. She couldn't even stand his cologne. What made him think buying a ring would change her mind about him? He was such an idiot.

"No. This was a mistake." He had turned to leave when he heard the man chuckle.

"Boy, if I had a dollar for every chum who walked in and then lost his nerve."

Harrison waited for the man to finish, but it never came. He turned to face him. "You'd be rich?"

The man laughed. "Well, I'd have a few dollars."

Harrison couldn't help but smile at the man.

He motioned Harrison over. "Look, either you love her, or you don't. It's that simple. If you do, what are you waiting for?"

If only it were that simple. He loved her, he knew that. But how would she react to hearing it? He could have sworn she felt something when they kissed. How could she not have? The chemistry between them sizzled. And the time they spent together…he'd thought it meant something.

But these last couple of days she'd been acting funny. And with her new rules, he was more confused than ever. What should he do?

He stared down at the rings. "Could I see the one on the left?"

∽

*P*enny glanced over at Harrison for the tenth time that evening. Something was wrong, but she couldn't weasel it out of him. After shopping at the mall he seemed more preoccupied than usual. He kept tugging on his shirt collar like it was choking him. No one else seemed to notice as the family sat around the living room enjoying another round of Harrison's eggnog.

Her father set his glass down on the end table. "So how long are you two going to wait to give me a grandson?"

Penny nearly spat out a mouthful of eggnog. "Daddy!"

Harrison suddenly had something caught in his throat and had to leave the room.

Kimmy whacked their father. "You embarrassed him."

Her father laughed. "It's a legitimate question."

A question for which Penny had no answer. Well, the truth was they'd never give him a grandson, but she couldn't say that. She just shifted uncomfortably until Harrison came back and sat next to her on the loveseat.

"So what's your favorite Christmas memory?" Harrison looked around the room.

Penny's warm cheeks grew even hotter. He was trying to change the subject. Save her some embarrassment, but he didn't realize the can of worms he was opening.

Her father grinned, and she knew what was coming. "It would have to be the time Penny fell asleep at the Christmas play."

The whole family busted up laughing, and Harrison's eyebrows knit together. "Why is that funny?"

Her father leaned forward. "Because she was *in* the play."

Clay joined in. "She was a shepherd. She almost fell off the stage!"

"You were too little to even remember it." Kimmy frowned.

"That doesn't make it any less funny." Clay went back to playing with his phone.

Harrison cleared his throat. "Well, I was thinking more along the lines—"

"Have you heard about the blind date incident?" Her father wasn't going to stop. Penny sank into the chair.

Harrison shook his head.

"Penny spent all day getting ready for a blind date. When the doorbell rang, she greeted the man, and even though he was older than she'd thought he'd be, she politely took his arm and started to lead him down to his car. Turned out, he was a door-to-door salesman trying to peddle household cleaner."

Penny covered her face with her hands as everyone laughed. Yep. Penny's big mess-ups. Her family's favorite pastime was reliving all the embarrassing things she'd ever done. At least they didn't know the biggest one yet. She waited through a couple more stories before she couldn't stand it anymore. "Excuse me," she said, and headed to the bathroom.

Her vision blurred as she tried to get a hold of her emotions. So what if she was the family screw-up. Who cared if Harrison was going to hear all about her stupid mistakes? She'd already told him plenty on her own.

She splashed water on her face and patted it dry with the hand towel. It was dumb to hide out in the bathroom. She took a deep breath and opened the door. As she walked down the hall, Harrison's voice carried.

"You know these stories hurt her, right?"

She froze.

Harrison continued. "Penny is a bright, compassionate woman with many strengths."

Penny's heart expanded and she took a step back.

Her father spoke. "She knows we're just kidding around."

"I know you don't mean anything by it," Harrison said. "But you have no idea the lengths she's gone through over the last two weeks to prove to you guys she's not just a screw-up. Bringing up all her past mistakes is only going to make her feel terrible."

"William's right," her mother said. "We could be hurting Penny's feelings."

Penny blinked back more tears. No one had ever defended her like that before. Harrison might possibly be the most considerate man she'd ever met. Most of the time her dates would join right in, laughing along with everyone else.

She waited in the shadow of the hallway until the conversation changed to talk about Christmas Eve. As she walked toward the living room, Harrison rounded the corner and she ran into the solid wall of his chest. "Oh!"

He grabbed her arms. "Sorry. I was coming to check on you. Are you okay?"

Her hands splayed on his chest, and the smell of his laundry detergent mixed with his own scent made her dizzy. She nodded. "I'm fine."

His heart beat under her fingers and she couldn't breathe. He gazed down at her and time slowed.

"Hey, look!" Kimmy's voice broke the trance she was in and she jumped back from Harrison. Kimmy grinned at them. "You guys are under the mistletoe."

Penny looked up, and sure enough, someone had hung a sprig of mistletoe in the hallway.

Kimmy winked at her. "Guess there's only one thing for you to do."

Harrison's eyes widened as if he'd rather kiss a bull. Penny's heart stopped for a moment and she sent her sister a silent plea. Kimmy put her hands on her hips and frowned. "Come on, William. Kiss her."

Harrison leaned over and gave her a tiny peck on the cheek.

Kimmy snorted. "That's not a kiss. Give her a real one."

The apology in Harrison's eyes was evident, even as he took his finger and lifted her chin. Her heart pounded against her ribcage as his lips came closer.

"Sorry," He whispered, his breath tickling her skin.

"It's okay," she whispered back, breathless.

His lips captured hers. The kiss started slow and soft, but she soon found herself on her tiptoes to get closer. His arms wrapped around her, pulling her to him. She'd been wrong to demand he back off. This kiss was like nothing she'd ever experienced before, and her nerve endings became aware of every sensation. She entwined her fingers in his hair.

She suddenly never wanted to stop kissing him. But she knew if she didn't stop soon, it would become awkward with Kimmy standing there gawking at them. She pulled back. Harrison stared at her, his eyes holding a silent question.

Kimmy fanned her face. "Wow, you two know how to kiss."

Her mother came around the corner. "What are you guys doing in the hallway?"

Kimmy pointed up, and her mother grinned. "Ah, so that's where you hung it. Don't let me interrupt the fun. I'm just heading to bed."

"Me too." Kimmy followed their mother, giving Penny a wide grin before turning the corner. They were alone again.

"Penny, I—"

"No, let me." Penny took a breath. If she didn't get it out now, she'd never have the nerve to say it. "I'm sorry I said those things the other night. I wasn't thinking clearly."

He squinted his eyes, as if he wasn't sure what she meant, so she pressed forward. "I didn't mean for you to be afraid to get near me." She forced a laugh. "I mean, we *are* supposed to be in love."

He nodded slowly. "Yes."

"It would be ridiculous for us to…" She looked down at her hands now gripping his biceps. "Not even touch."

He stood silent for a moment, studying her, his arms still around her. "Of course."

She made the mistake of looking into his eyes. Even in the dim hallway, the icy blue depths drew her in, and made her knees go weak. She turned away. "We'd better go upstairs."

"Yes. It's late." He stepped back and she instantly missed the feel of his arms around her.

CHAPTER 22

Harrison patted his pocket for the umpteenth time that day making sure the ring box was still there, and hadn't burned a hole in his trousers. Why was he doing this to himself? For heaven's sake, he met Penny a couple of weeks ago. There's no way she would agree to stay married to him. They barely knew each other. This was insane.

"Would you like more ham?" Marci looked at him expectantly. "You haven't eaten much."

Harrison shook his head. "No, thank you. It was delicious, but I can't take another bite." That was an understatement. His stomach churned and he regretted all the other bites he'd forced down throughout the day.

They'd gotten family photos taken that morning. Turned out the photographer was a family friend who had a studio set up in his basement. He took photos of the entire family, then singled out Harrison and Penny for a few newlywed photos. Harrison was sure they would have turned out better had he not been fretting the entire time.

Today was Christmas Eve. Just one more day, and they'd

be back in California with Patrice. He'd have to confess to Penny he had his trust fund, and it was depleted. He ran his hand over the lump in his pocket, unsure of what to do.

Everyone stood to clean the table. Harrison picked up several glasses and took them to the dishwasher. Marci laid a hand on his. "Thank you, William. You're so considerate." Her eyes misted over. "We're lucky to have you as a part of this family. Thank you for making my daughter happy."

A pain stabbed at his chest. He hadn't expected to feel this guilty deceiving Penny's family. They didn't even know his real name. "That's kind of you to say."

Marci finished filling the dishwasher and everyone congregated in the living room. Harrison wasn't sure if he should put his arm around Penny or not. He finally settled on resting it on the back of the loveseat.

"It's our tradition to open family gifts on Christmas Eve. Then Santa comes while we sleep." The way Marci beamed made Harrison smile. "Clay, will you pass out the gifts?"

There weren't an extraordinary number of presents under the tree, and the wrapping paper didn't look expensive, but for some reason Harrison felt an anticipation he hadn't felt in years. Maybe it was the joy on everyone's faces as they chatted and passed around the goodies he and Penny had made. Or perhaps it was the family atmosphere.

They took turns opening gifts—small inexpensive items, but everyone expressed their warm thanks, and the tone was so different from what he was used to. When it was Harrison's turn to open his gift from Penny, he was surprised to find an herb garden kit. He'd always wanted to try growing his own herbs, but had never told anyone. He turned to Penny. "How did you know?"

She laughed and poked him in the side. "All foodies want to grow their own herbs."

"Thank you." The thoughtfulness of the gift touched him,

and he leaned over and gave her a kiss before he could think about it. Surprise showed on her face for a quick second before she masked it.

A knock sounded on the door and Marci stood. When she opened the door, Kimmy sucked in a breath. Her boyfriend stood on the steps.

"Good evening, ma'am. I'm Rob Curtis and I've been dating your daughter."

Kimmy ran to the door. "What are you doing?"

Arthur got up from his chair. "What's going on?"

Marci put her hand to her heart and backed away from the door. Kimmy shut the front door in Rob's face, turned and pressed her back against it. She stretched out her arms, as if that would block everyone from what had just happened.

"Kimmy?" Arthur's voice boomed. "What is the meaning of this? Surely you're not dating that hooligan."

"Arthur!" Marci scolded.

Visible guilt dripped from Kimmy like oil. Her gaze bounced all around the room. "Um…"

Another knock came from the door.

"Well don't make him stand outside in the snow." Clay crossed the room and shoved Kimmy out of the way. He opened the door. "Come on in."

Rob hesitantly stepped inside. He ran his hand over his shaved head. "I'm sorry to interrupt your evening. I just have one thing that needs to be said, and then I'll leave."

Kimmy stood silent.

Rob pressed on, turning toward Arthur. "I love your daughter. I know I've made mistakes, but I've spent the last ten years making them right. I might not ever be good enough for Kim, but if she'll have me, I've come to ask her hand in marriage."

He swiveled to Kimmy, sank to one knee and pulled out a

ring from his leather jacket. Kimmy's eyes grew until Harrison worried they'd pop out of her head.

"Will you marry me?"

She threw her arms around his neck. "Yes! Yes, I'll marry you!"

The room erupted in commotion, everyone talking at once. Marci shouted at Arthur, and Arthur looked like he was going to blow a gasket, while Clay seemed to be enjoying the show. Penny's face drained of color.

Kimmy stood and shouted, "Stop!"

The room went silent. Kimmy swallowed, took a deep breath, and faced her parents. "Look, I didn't want to tell you I was dating Rob, but we are in love. And getting married!" She squealed, then settled down. "I know you don't approve, but this is how it is. You'll have to accept it." She squared her shoulders and stared down the room in a silent challenge.

Everyone stood stunned until Penny jumped up and hugged her. "Congratulations."

Arthur's face turned dark red. "I don't want any daughter of mine—"

"Daddy," Kimmy interrupted. "It's Christmas. Let's talk about this later. Can't we just have Christmas?"

"But—"

"Arthur," Marci said. "Kimmy's right. Let's continue with our evening. We can talk later." Marci pointed to where Kimmy had been on the couch. "Rob, why don't you join us?"

The tension in the room didn't dissipate, but as everyone sat down the frown on Arthur's face lessened. They resumed the present opening, and Clay passed a plate of cookies to Rob.

Penny opened her gift from Harrison next. It was a pair of TARDIS earrings he'd picked up at the convention and managed to hide from her. She bounced in her seat like a kid. "I love them! Thank you, Harrison!"

He froze, waiting to see if anyone noticed she'd called him by a different name, his heart hammering in his chest.

Kimmy spoke first. "Did you say Harrison?"

Penny's face flamed red. "I, uh…"

Clay put his phone down. "Wait, this isn't William?"

"He…um…" Penny fiddled with the wrapping paper, looking down at her lap.

Harrison had to say something. Anything. They all stared at him. He cleared his throat. "It's my fault. I used my last name online, and Penny mistook it for my first. She started calling me William and it stuck. But my name is really Harrison." The lie seemed believable. It wasn't that he wanted to deceive Penny's family, but he'd rather do that than admit the truth and watch Penny be humiliated.

No one said anything, and heat crept up Harrison's neck.

Arthur stared at him, a puzzled expression on his face. "Harrison, as in Harrison Williams?"

"Yes."

"I wish someone would have told me we were calling you by the wrong name," Marci said, frowning. "I'm not quite sure why Penny didn't say anything…"

"She was afraid of being made fun of." Harrison didn't mean for it to come out as an accusation.

"Well." Marci's smile was forced. "It's not a big deal."

Arthur shifted in his seat. "Harrison Williams, as in CEO of Harrison Williams Investment Group?"

Harrison wished another person would burst in and propose to take the attention off himself. "Yes."

Kimmy laughed. "Get out. You married a CEO?"

Penny turned a deeper shade of red, which he didn't think was possible. "I'm sorry we lied," she said quietly.

Clay stared at his phone, his eyes growing wide. "Oh man, you're a billionaire?"

Technically he was worth billions, but only because he'd

inherit a billion dollar company when Patrice died. Right now he was cash poor. Harrison tugged at his collar, feeling like a broken record. "Yeah."

An awkward pause settled in until Clay said, "Hot da—"

"Clay!" Marci said.

"I was going to say dang."

Marci scowled at Clay, then plastered on a smile. "Well, we're almost done. Who's opening next?"

~

Harrison lay on the floor listening to Penny's even breathing. Well, that had been uncomfortable, but they'd gotten through it. Penny's family had accepted the lie, and no one suspected her real mistake.

He pulled out the ring box and opened it. The diamond he'd picked wasn't large and flashy. It was understated, but elegant, like everything else Penny wore.

"Are you awake?"

Penny's voice startled him and he snapped the ring box shut and stuffed it under his blanket. She wasn't looking down at him. Maybe she hadn't seen it. "Yeah. Just thinking."

She exhaled. "I can't sleep either." The bed made a noise and her face popped over the edge. "Sorry about earlier. I can't believe I messed up and said your name."

"It's okay. It all worked out."

"Yeah, thanks." Her face looked troubled. "Sorry to put you on the spot. I hope it didn't make things awkward for you."

"It's fine."

The bed creaked again and her face disappeared. "My family can be a little overwhelming."

He smiled despite the awkwardness. Her family was

warm and friendly, and even though they had flaws, they made him feel at home. "They're perfect."

"Ha. You're drunk."

"No, seriously. You've met my family, right?"

Penny snort-laughed. "Okay, compared to Patrice, my house is full of angels."

Harrison's smile faded. "They don't mean to hurt you, when they tease you about things."

Penny's voice came back, soft. "I know." After a moment of silence, Penny said, "Why is Patrice the way she is?"

Harrison squinted in the dark, trying to see beyond the pale shadows. "She's very insecure. She wasn't well received when she married my father."

Penny looked down at him again. "What happened to your mother?"

"She died when I was young. Cancer. I barely remember her."

She reached out and took his hand, warmth spreading over him. "I'm sorry."

"It's okay. Like I said, I barely remember her."

"It must have been hard, having Patrice come and replace her."

Harrison squeezed Penny's hand. "Patrice let our nanny raise me. Lucy Perkins was her name, and she was everything Patrice was not. She became like a mother to me."

"What happened to her?"

Harrison swallowed the lump in his throat. "Patrice fired her when I was twelve. Accused her of stealing, although I always suspected she was insanely jealous of our relationship. Lucy packed up and I haven't seen her since."

Penny sucked in a sharp breath. "That's terrible."

"It is what it is."

"Well, you're right. My family is pretty awesome." She pulled her hand away.

"How do you feel about your sister marrying Rob?"

Penny made a face. "I still don't like it, but you've made a good point. I have to support her, or it will drive us apart."

"Maybe he's changed."

"Yeah. Maybe." Penny paused. "What are you going to do once you have your trust fund? I mean, I know you're going to move into a nice house, but have you ever thought about leaving the investment group? Doing something you love?"

He knew what she was getting at, and truth be told he had thought about it. But it could never happen, especially now that Patrice had drained his account. "I can't open a restaurant. I can't leave the firm."

"I know your dad wanted you to run it, but couldn't someone else do that?"

"If I left, Patrice would be furious. She'd probably write me out of the will."

She patted his arm. "But you'd be happy." She rolled over, letting the words sink in. Penny really didn't care about his money. She'd rather he be happy and broke than a billionaire stuck in a life she hated. She had more courage than he did. He didn't think he could walk away from it all.

"Good night, Harrison."

"Good night."

CHAPTER 23

Penny sat at the breakfast table with her parents, pushing cereal around in a pool of milk with her spoon. It was Christmas Day and all she could think about was how her family thought she was happily married to Harrison. She'd gotten what she asked for. No one knew she'd messed up. So why did it feel so sour?

Harrison sat in the chair next to hers and gave her a smile. He looked like a model from a magazine, which didn't make her feel any better. She stared down at her bowl and tried to push the horrible feelings away.

"You okay?" her mother asked.

"Fine," she lied. She couldn't tell anyone otherwise. What was wrong with her? She'd gotten away with her fake marriage. They would be leaving that evening, and no one would have to know the truth. She should have been elated, but instead she couldn't eat because her stomach felt like it was full of rocks.

Kimmy slid into the chair across from her and set a bowl down with a clink. "Who died?"

Penny forced a smile. "No one. Sorry, I was just thinking."

"Well you'd better stop or you're going to depress everyone." Kimmy poured her milk and then passed it to Harrison. "What Christmas movies are we watching today?"

"*It's a Wonderful Life* is playing all day on the History channel," Harrison said.

"Oh, I love that one." Kimmy shoved a bite of cereal in her mouth.

The ring on Kimmy's finger caught the light and Penny's mood worsened. Even though she didn't like Rob, her sister was happy. Getting married. She'd found love.

All Penny had was a bogus relationship that would dissolve soon, and an overwhelming urge to throw up.

"Hey, I've been thinking," Kimmy said with her mouth full. She swallowed. "You two met in a chat room for *Doctor Who* fans, right? But you—" She pointed at Harrison. "Yesterday you said you're not really into that. What were you doing there?"

"I...uh..." Harrison's wide eyes turned to Penny.

"He was messing around online. Clicking on different things." It was lame, but it was all Penny could come up with on the spot.

"And I was also thinking...Penny said your last name was Tucker. Where did that come from?" Kimmy stared at Harrison, whose face drained of color.

"Well, um..." Harrison coughed into his fist.

Everyone around the table stared at Harrison, and Penny knew this wouldn't work. If they lied now, she'd have to lie forever. Even after they divorced and Harrison went away, she'd forever be lying to her family. She could barely take another second.

"I lied," she blurted.

As soon as she said it, she wished the words back in her mouth, but it was too late. Her parents looked at her with disappointment. They didn't even know the half of it yet.

And she had to tell them. There was no way she could get away with this. How had she ever thought this was a good idea?

But as she sat there with her family looking at her, she lost her nerve. The room grew impossibly hot and she stood. "Excuse me."

She ran upstairs to her room.

∽

Harrison sat there frozen, his spoon hanging in mid-air. What was Penny thinking? He slowly set his spoon down.

"What did she mean, she lied?" Marci's face was stony.

What should he tell them? He wasn't sure what she meant. "I don't know. I'd better go talk to her." His chair scraped the floor as he stood.

He climbed the stairs and entered Penny's small room. She was on the bed, her head in her hands. He eased down next to her and put his hand on her back. "What's going on?"

She didn't move for a moment before she faced him. He thought maybe she was crying, but her eyes were dry. "I can't do this anymore. I want out."

Pain stabbed in his chest. Was she saying what he thought she was saying? He needed her to clarify. "Out?"

"Yes. I'm done." Penny picked at her bedspread. "I need to get on with my life."

Harrison's mind reeled. Penny was ready to get a divorce and go separate ways. Panic filled him and he glanced at his pillow where the ring was hidden.

Penny continued. "This was a bad idea. I shouldn't have agreed to do this in the first place."

Great. She regretted the last two weeks with him. Here he

was falling in love with her, and she was wishing the whole thing hadn't happened. "I'm sorry."

Penny avoided his gaze. "It's not your fault. I just need to be done. Maybe you can call your attorney and see how the trust fund is going."

Guilt for not telling Penny crept up into his chest. "He called. Patrice surrendered the funds."

"Really? That's great news." Penny smiled, although it didn't reach her eyes. Her face grew sober. "There's no reason for me to go to California with you, then."

The words smacked him in the face. She couldn't wait to get away from him. "I guess not. I'll get your check ready." Except he didn't have enough. He'd have to pay her half of what he owed until he could straighten out what Patrice did with the rest of the money.

Penny shook her head. "I changed my mind. I don't want it."

She...didn't want the money? Harrison didn't understand. How would she get on with her life without it? "What do you mean?"

"This whole thing was a mistake. I wouldn't feel right taking your money."

Figures. The first girl he found that didn't care about his money didn't care about him either. He wiped his palms on his pants, unable to look at her. "What will you do?"

"Get a job here I guess. Live with my parents until I get back on my feet. Maybe con someone into going with me to get my car at the Las Vegas airport." Penny took in a deep breath and let it out slowly. "I'm going to tell my parents. Everything."

He'd assumed that was where she was going with this. And a part of him admired her for owning up to her mistake instead of hiding it. She had come to terms with it and realized the truth was better than keeping up with the lies. An urge to support her came over him. "We can tell them together."

Another small smile formed on her lips. "Thanks, I appreciate the offer, but I need to do this myself."

"You can tell them. I'll just come with you for moral support."

She slowly nodded. "Okay."

He got up and held out his hand to her. "Let's go get this over with."

As they descended the stairs, he tried to ignore the way her hand sent zaps of electricity up his arm. They'd be saying good-bye in a few minutes. He had to face reality. It was over.

∽

Penny gathered her family in the living room, her nerves shot. They were going to have so much fun with this one. Stories of this would be told at family events for years to come. She didn't even want to think of what would happen this summer at the Ackerman family reunion. Aunt Ida's horse-laugh filled her mind.

She glanced around the room and cleared her throat. "I want to tell you something, but please wait until I'm done to say anything."

Her mother twisted her hands together, a look of concern on her face. "Of course, dear."

Kimmy nudged Clay and motioned for him to put away his phone. Clay rolled his eyes but stuffed his cell in his pocket.

Penny wiped her hands on her jeans. "Harrison and I got married by accident."

Confusion swept over her father's features. "What do you mean?"

"The man I was chatting with online was named William. He asked me to marry him, and I accepted, but he stood me up at the altar. The limo driver picked up the wrong guy." She made a lame gesture toward Harrison sitting beside her.

Clay made a snort-laugh and picked up a magazine to hide behind.

She steeled herself for the laughter and the jabs, but when no one else said anything, she continued. "I was so embarrassed that I'd made such a colossal mistake, I asked him to come home with me and pretend to be William."

Clay shook with laughter. "Oh, man, that's—" Kimmy pinched his arm. "Ouch!"

"Shut up!" Kimmy hissed.

Penny's tongue felt like sandpaper in her mouth and heat flamed her face. "No, go ahead and laugh. It's funny."

After she'd given them permission to laugh, the room grew silent. Her mother tugged at the hem of her shirt. "You...aren't really married?"

How could she explain? This was too complicated. "No, we're married."

"But, you're not in love?" Her mother blinked like she was going to cry.

Oh, dear. She expected laughter, not tears. The look on her mother's face stabbed a knife into her chest. And what a question. She had strong feelings for Harrison, but how could she talk about them when she didn't understand them herself? She took a deep breath, and decided to go with the simple answer, even if it wasn't altogether true. "No."

She thought Harrison winced, but when she turned, his face was unreadable.

Her father looked like he wanted to punch someone. "You mean you...and he..."

She also wasn't prepared for anger. "I'm sorry, Daddy."

"What were you thinking?" her father said, one decibel lower than a shout.

Her mother wiped a tear from her cheek. "Are you going to get a divorce?"

The pit of her stomach hardened. "Yes."

An uncomfortable silence settled in the room, and Penny shifted in her seat. "I'm sorry, I shouldn't have tried to cover up my mistake."

Another span of awkward silence stretched out. "Well," her mother finally said. "Thank you for telling us the truth. It couldn't have been easy for you."

Her father still looked like he wanted to hurt someone, and Penny wasn't sure if his anger was directed at her or Harrison. Maybe both. Just to be safe, she tugged on Harrison's arm and they stood. "We've decided it's best if Harrison goes back to California alone."

Her mother looked down at her lap. "That's wise."

"I'm going to go help him pack." Penny practically dragged Harrison out of the room and up the stairs. When they got back in the bedroom she leaned up against the door and swiped a hand over her face. "Glad that's over."

Harrison looked like he wanted to say something, but he stayed silent. Instead, he pulled out his suitcase and started packing.

Seeing him getting ready to leave sent her heart into a near panic. She'd been so focused on clearing up the lie that she hadn't thought about Harrison leaving. About never seeing him again. Her stomach clenched. "Do you…need any help?"

Oh, why had she said that? It sounded like she was shoving him out the door. Like she couldn't wait for him to leave. Nerves assaulted her and she had to wipe the sweat off her hands.

"No."

He glanced at her, and her breath caught. He was leaving. Really going, and she didn't want him to. In fact, an incredible urge surged in her to grab hold of him and give him another sucker-fish kiss until he fell in love with her.

He shoved items into his case while she fretted about what to do. Should she tell him she loved him? Did she love him? Her feelings had been so mixed up since William broke her heart, she wasn't sure. All she knew was she had this horrible empty feeling in the pit of her stomach watching him pack.

Harrison had his trust fund now. He didn't need her. He'd be better off without her dragging him down, embarrassing his family. Marrying her had been a mistake. He'd wanted some rich girl. Someone who could step into his world and make him look good.

She was not that someone.

He'd probably go back to living in that mansion, going to fancy parties. Maybe he'd meet a girl. He deserved to be happy. Thoughts swirled around in her head, making her dizzy, and she sat down on her bed.

Harrison zipped up his suitcase. "That's everything."

"I'll...uh...see you to the door." She followed him down the stairs and across the living room.

He opened the door and stepped out onto the front stoop, then turned to her. "Penny—"

"Harrison—" She interrupted. "Sorry, you go first."

He shook his head. "No, you."

She swallowed the lump forming in her throat. She wanted to tell him to wait, that she'd made another mistake, and she wanted to go back with him. But it wouldn't be right. "I just wanted to tell you...to have a safe trip."

He nodded. "I will."

The cold December air brushed past her and she knew

she had to close the door soon. "Bye." The word almost choked her.

"Bye, Penny."

He turned to go and she gripped the door. "Wait!"

Slowly he faced her. "Yes?"

Her heart beat so loud she worried he'd hear it. "You didn't tell me what you were going to say."

He appeared contemplative for a moment. "I was just going to wish you luck, in finding a job and everything."

Her heart sank. She was hoping he was going to say something else. Something like, "I'll miss you." Or, "I've enjoyed the last two weeks." Or maybe, "I love you more than life itself."

She lowered her gaze. "Okay. Thanks."

He gave her a quick nod, then turned and walked to his rental car. He loaded his things, got in, and started the engine. Her chest grew heavy as he pulled out of the driveway. She watched his car disappear down the road.

CHAPTER 24

Harrison bit into the stale vending machine sandwich and stared at the sea of people walking by him as he waited for his plane. The hollow feeling in his chest expanded. Leaving Penny had been the hardest thing he'd had to do in his life. Even confessing their deception to her parents paled in comparison.

It was hard to believe he'd only met her two weeks ago. She'd become so much a part of his life in that short time. She'd brought laughter to his world. Everything came alive when she was around. Even him. And now she was gone.

His stomach soured and he tossed the rest of his sandwich in the trash. He needed to forget about Penny. She didn't feel the same way about him. He had to move on.

Shifting his focus, he geared up for his confrontation with Patrice. She'd had no right to touch his trust fund. Sure, she had set up the account and was the trustee, so she had total control of it. But his father had made it clear he wanted that money to go to Harrison and his brother when they were stable adults. Patrice knew his father's wishes.

There had been thirty million dollars in there. His

brother had taken fifteen two years ago when he'd gotten married. Where had the rest gone?

Was she hiding it in another account? He couldn't imagine her doing that. She was cold and impersonal, but she wasn't a thief. He could see her dipping into the account to carry on appearances, though. She was obsessed with keeping up with the neighbors.

His flight was called and he stood and grabbed his case. The truth would come out soon enough. He wasn't going to let Patrice off the hook.

When his plane arrived in L.A., he got in his car and sped along the freeway. The radio blared the music Penny liked, and he turned it off in frustration.

By the time he got home, it was late and the house was dark, but he was determined to confront Patrice. He set his suitcases down and walked toward his stepmother's room. He pounded on the door, the sound echoing through the hall.

He heard stirring, and then footsteps. Her door opened. She wore her nightgown, but didn't look surprised to see him. "Harrison." Her tone was cold, but also held a tired edge to it.

"I need to speak to you."

She hesitated for only a moment. "Come on in." She motioned for him to sit in the reading chair.

"I assume you know why I'm here."

Patrice had no make-up on, and her age showed. She nodded. "The trust fund." She folded her arms under her chest.

"Where's the money?"

"Gone."

So, she had spent it. Anger pulsed through him. "It wasn't yours to spend!"

She sank down to the bed, her shoulders drooping. "I know." She twisted a tissue in her hands.

Even though she looked pathetic, he wasn't going to let her get away with what she'd done. "I demand an explanation."

She stared down at the tissue. "I...I've been paying for Antonio's medical treatment."

Harrison blinked. If she'd said she'd been taking belly dancing classes he wouldn't have been more surprised. He didn't even know Antonio was ill. "What?"

Patrice turned toward the window. "Antonio's been getting cancer treatments for the last three years. He couldn't pay for it." She paused, and he waited for her to continue. "It's my fault."

"How is his cancer your fault?"

She sighed. "Not the cancer. The lack of medical insurance."

Harrison shifted in his chair. "I see." Had she lost her mind? It wasn't her fault, and she definitely didn't have any liability. Why had she been paying his medical bills?

"I..." She cleared her throat. "I loved your father."

That came out of left field. Where was she going with that?

She stared down at her hands. "After he died I got lonely. Antonio and I..."

Oh, crud. He knew where she was headed now. He held up a hand. "Stop. I don't want to hear any more."

"His diagnosis came not long after we got involved. I couldn't stand to lose him as well."

Harrison shook his head. "There was fifteen million in there. His medical bills couldn't have been that high."

Patrice swallowed, her face turning green. "When I realized I'd spent over two million dollars, I panicked. I tried to get the money back by investing in some risky stocks."

The way she fidgeted, he knew there was more, so he waited for her to continue.

"The more money I lost, the more risk I took, trying to get it back." She looked like she was going to throw up. "I invested the last three million right before you married Penny. The company went belly up last week."

All that money. Gone. Harrison's mouth dried out. How could she have done that? Anger pulsed through him. She should have just told him instead of trying to cover up her mistake. The realization hit him that he and Penny had done the exact same thing.

"What about your money? Dad left you a sizable amount."

She dabbed at her eye. "I thought I was being wise by investing the bulk of it into Harrison Williams stocks. But the company has been going down, and I've lost a lot. I can't sell now. I'd lose so much."

His anger dissipated. There was still money tied up in the business. All he had to do was pull things around. He ran his hand through his hair. "Okay. I guess that's it then."

Patrice's head snapped up. "Okay? That's all you're going to say?"

"You obviously didn't mean to drain the account. What else is there to say?"

She straightened her back. "I'll get you your money. After the firm's stocks go back up."

He had no choice but to agree to it. "Okay."

"Trent and I were talking. He's been going into the office while you were gone. He has some ideas for turning the business around."

"Trent?" The notion seemed absurd.

"He actually has some good ideas."

Harrison shrugged. "I'll talk to him tomorrow."

Patrice smoothed her nightgown, back to her pious posture. "You do that. This business is all we have left."

"And you've got to rein in your spending."

Her mouth tightened into a thin line. "You will not disrespect me."

"I mean no disrespect. But you can't act like we have money when we don't."

She blanched and didn't say anything else.

He leaned back in his chair and studied her. "Why didn't you tell me about you and Antonio?"

"No one must know," she said so low it was almost a whisper.

"You'd rather keep up appearances than be happy?"

She stood. "I don't expect you to understand. But I do expect you to keep this information to yourself. The only reason I told you in the first place was because I owed you an explanation about your trust fund."

"But—"

"It's late and I'm sure Penny is wondering where you are."

The mention of Penny sent his stomach to his toes and reminded him why his chest felt hollow. What was he going to tell her? He couldn't pretend they were still happily married. He stared at his shoes. "Penny's gone."

A smirk landed on her face. "Found out there's no money, did she? Then I did you a favor."

Harrison clenched his hands into fists. "It wasn't like that." He stormed out of her room and slammed the door.

CHAPTER 25

Penny lay on the couch, staring at the television and not seeing it. She snuggled into the afghan her Aunt Tilly had made and sniffled. Kimmy had gone back to college. Her father was at work, her mother out shopping, and her brother wasn't due home from school for another hour.

Plenty of time to wallow in self-pity on the couch. She pulled another tissue from the box and wiped her nose. He hadn't called. Even though she'd tossed her cell phone, she'd been hoping he'd at least call the house. But…nothing. Phone silence, for two weeks.

If there had been any doubt in her mind about how he felt, it was gone now. He didn't feel the same. Not the way she felt about him.

She loved him.

And she'd messed it all up. Again. She was such a failure. No job. Living in her parents' house. She looked down at her sweat pants. She couldn't even muster up the strength to get dressed in the morning.

What a waste of skin she was. Harrison would be better

off with someone else. He deserved a girl who could make him happy. Someone who would stand up to Patrice and help him leave his horrible job.

The front door rattled and her mother entered, her arms full of groceries. Concern washed over her face. "Penny, can you help?"

She groaned inwardly but rose from the couch anyway. "Yes." She dumped the afghan in a heap.

"Take this one, will you?" Her mother held out a brown paper bag.

Penny grabbed it and grunted. "This is heavy. What's in it?"

"Oh, sorry. There are cans in the bottom."

They went into the kitchen and emptied the bags onto the laminate counter, putting things in the cupboard. Her mother eyed her. "How are you doing?"

Penny sighed. She'd known this conversation would be coming. Her mother had been giving her 'the eye' for a while now. "I'm fine, Mom."

Her mother pulled a can of corn from the bag and placed it on the shelf. "Fine?" She raised one eyebrow in an 'oh, really?' kind of way.

"All right. I guess I've been…moody lately." Maybe that would satisfy her.

"Honey, I think we need to talk."

Annoyance pinched her, and she frowned. "We are talking."

"Then tell me. Have you realized yet that you love him?" Her mother's bold challenge came with a firm stance and hands on her hips.

Great. Her mother knew. Penny swiped a strand of hair out of her face. No use in denying it. "Yes."

Her mother gave her a sympathetic look. "How long have you known?"

Penny's shoulders slumped. "I don't know. I guess ever since he left."

"And what are you going to do about it?"

Gah! Why couldn't a hole open up in the kitchen floor so she could jump into it? Heat seared Penny's cheeks. "Nothing."

"Why not?" Her mother picked up a gallon of milk and opened the fridge.

"He only married me to get his trust fund money."

Her mother slowly closed the refrigerator. "I see." She studied Penny for a moment. "What would happen if you called him and told him how you felt?"

She'd gone over that in her mind a thousand times. In her fantasies, she flew to California and told him in person. She looked amazing, of course, and he pulled her into his arms and kissed her. In reality, he'd probably laugh at her. "I don't know."

"Well, you won't find out unless you do tell him."

Heh, easy for her mother to say. She was already married to the love of her life. She wasn't the one taking the risk of being laughed at. Besides, he would have called if he had the same feelings, right?

The sting of being rejected was too much, and Penny blinked back tears. "He doesn't want me. I just need to move on."

Her mother looked sad for a moment, then brushed it off. "All right, then. Someone called looking for you." She dug around in her purse then held out a piece of paper.

Penny grabbed it and read it. The room spun. "The Tribute Show? They're back on?"

"Yes. They want you to come immediately."

Her heart pounded in her chest. She had a job! And not just some stupid fast food gig, she had her show back. "Mom, this is great news. Why didn't you tell me right away?"

"I wanted to talk to you about the more important issue first."

"More important? Are you crazy? This is my career. This is more important."

A sort of sad look flitted across her mother's face. "Are you sure?"

Penny stopped. Her mother was right. As exciting as it was to have her show back, Penny knew her relationship with Harrison was infinitely more important to her. She'd gladly give up the show if it meant she could be happy with him forever.

But it just wasn't going to happen. He was filing for a divorce. She'd probably get the papers in the mail any day now. And it wasn't fair for her to force her affections on him. Heaven only knew how many girls did that to him already.

"You're right, Mom. But since I'm pining after someone I can't have, I need to get on with my life. And this is the perfect thing to distract me." She waved the paper. "I'm going to go call them, then make flight arrangements." She sprinted out of the room.

Her mother called after her. "They already have plane tickets for you."

CHAPTER 26

Harrison leaned over his desk examining the paperwork Trent had given him. The numbers looked good. They were only projections, but because of the changes Trent had made, things were starting to look up.

It had been two months since he'd left Penny in Iowa, and not a day had gone by that he hadn't thought about her. Wondered what she was doing. Wished he could call her just to hear her voice.

He'd put off talking to his attorney about getting the divorce papers drawn up, because he was a fool and still held a small hope that she'd call and say she missed him. Idiot.

He'd gone ahead and moved into the apartment, which had probably been a mistake. Every evening he sat there, alone, thinking about Penny. But he couldn't bring himself to move out.

He sat back in his office chair and exhaled. Why was he torturing himself? It didn't do any good to dwell on thoughts of her. It only made the hole in his chest widen. He put his hands behind his head and closed his eyes. The room smelled of shoe polish and leather, smells that always used to comfort him. But not today. Everything in his life had turned flat since he and Penny had parted.

Trent walked into his office and plopped down on a chair. "What do you think?"

"These projections look really good. Where did you learn to do all this stuff?"

Trent snorted. "I took three and a half years of business school. Just because I didn't graduate doesn't mean I didn't learn anything."

Harrison felt like he was looking at Trent for the first time. "Why did you drop out of school?"

He scowled. "Because I wasn't wanted here."

"What makes you say that?"

Trent stretched his legs out in front of him. "I came home for Christmas my senior year. Dad was going on and on about how well you were doing at the firm. I pulled him aside and asked him what I was going to take over after I graduated. He said, 'Don't worry. Harrison has it. You can go do anything you want.' It was then that I realized it didn't matter what I did. I'd never measure up to you."

The words hit Harrison in the chest. "He didn't mean it like that."

"Maybe not. But it was clear he didn't see a place for me at the firm. So I quit school. Gave up."

"Well, I'm glad you're here now. You're pulling us out of a mess."

Trent smiled. "I have other ideas."

Harrison laughed. "Maybe you should take over."

Trent sobered and pulled his legs back. "I would like that."

"Really?"

The chair squeaked as Trent shifted his weight. "If I may be so blunt, you hate this job. Why don't you let me take over?"

Harrison was speechless. Trent wanted to take control of the company?

"I mean, it's none of my business but you come in every day and you look miserable. It's obvious you'd rather be doing anything else. I don't want to point fingers, but a CEO who doesn't want to be where he is can run an organization into the ground."

He was right. Harrison had been too blinded to see it before, but Trent had hit it exactly. It was Harrison's fault the company was suffering. His fault because he hated what he was doing. He swore under his breath.

"I didn't mean to offend you."

"No, you're right. I'm ruining the firm."

Trent rubbed his hands together. "Then let me take over. You go start up that restaurant, because I know that's what you really want to do."

Harrison frowned. He'd love nothing more. But how was he supposed to do that? "I can't. I have no start-up money."

"I'll fund it."

Harrison gripped the leather armrests of his office chair. "You'd do that?"

"Of course. You're my brother. And I can't stand to see you moping around here anymore."

Harrison ran his finger along the edge of his desk. He wanted to be happy. Starting up his own restaurant was his dream. But he couldn't muster up the enthusiasm.

"Why aren't you smiling?"

How could he explain how he was feeling to Trent? He barely understood it himself.

"It's that Las Vegas girl, isn't it? You fell in love with her." Trent loosened his tie, a grin on his face.

Harrison pulled the ring he'd purchased out of his pocket. He'd been carrying it around with him. Stupid. Carrying around a ring for a girl who wasn't even there. "I was going to propose."

"Oh, man. That's too good. Propose to your wife." He chuckled at his own little joke. "Why didn't you?"

The diamond caught the light. "She wanted out."

"Did you tell her how you feel?"

His throat grew tight. "No."

Trent stood up from his chair. "What are you waiting for? You've got to tell her."

Harrison let the ring drop to the papers on his desk, making a quiet thud. "She doesn't feel the same."

"How do you know? Did you ask her?"

The hollow feeling in Harrison's chest constricted. "I didn't have to."

"You know what they say about assuming." Trent picked up the ring. "If you don't tell her, I'm going to do it for you."

Harrison stood and swiped the ring from his brother's hand, glaring at him.

Trent grew serious. "Listen, I know it's none of my business, but let me tell you something. If you love her, you don't want to let her go."

The way he said it, like he was speaking from experience, gave Harrison pause. "What, you and Candy?"

Trent looked like he'd been deflated. "She's moved out. I messed everything up."

"You mean you really did love her?" No way. He was sure their marriage was fake.

"Of course I did." A scowl crossed Trent's face. "What did you think?"

"Nothing." Harrison knew better than to say what he thought.

"I've just been a jerk. But you're deflecting. We were talking about you and Penny. Looks like you fell hard."

Harrison plopped back down on his chair. Trent didn't

know the half of it. "I can't eat. I can't sleep. Penny is all I can think about."

Trent pointed to the door, a smirk on his face. "Then go to her."

The thought of seeing Penny again instantly lightened his mood. But what if she told him she didn't feel the same? Could he face rejection from her again? Inner conflict tugged him in two directions.

Trent leaned over and placed his hands on the desk. "Listen, you've got two choices. You can either sit around here and feel terrible, or you can go take a chance on the woman you love."

Once again, Trent was right. He had to go see Penny. He'd tried life without her, and ended up miserable. He had to let her know how he felt. "Okay. But do me a favor, would you?"

Trent nodded.

"Go talk to Candy."

Trent smiled. "I will."

Harrison pulled his rental car into the snow-covered Iowa driveway and cut the engine. The sun was low in the sky, casting long shadows over the street. It was a Friday evening. Maybe Penny wasn't home. Another thought caused him to freeze. What if she was out on a date?

He wouldn't know unless he went to the door. Gathering up his courage, he got out of the car and walked up the sidewalk to the steps. When he pressed the doorbell, he heard shuffling and then Marci stood before him.

She gasped. "Harrison? What are you doing here?"

"I need to see Penny."

A look of concern crossed Marci's face. "Is this about the divorce?"

"No. Well, sort of. Is she here?" Harrison tugged at his collar. This wasn't going as expected.

"You'd better come inside. It's freezing out there." Marci held the door open and Harrison entered.

Arthur craned his neck and nearly fell out of his recliner. "Harrison?"

"I'm here to speak to Penny."

Marci ushered him over to a chair. "Sit. Penny's not here."

Disappointment settled in his gut. "Where is she?"

"Gone. She went back to Las Vegas." Marci sat on the arm of the couch. "Did you fly all the way here to bring her the divorce papers?"

"No. I—" What was he going to say? He didn't even know what to say to Penny, not to mention her parents. His hands grew sweaty. "I just need to talk to her. Why is she back in Las Vegas?"

"She didn't tell you?" Marci and Arthur exchanged glances.

"She hasn't called. I haven't talked to her since..." He let his voice trail off. This was pathetic. Why did he let things get like this? He shouldn't have left her.

"She got a call from the people doing the tribute show. They wanted her back."

He smiled. "That's great. She loved doing that show." At least she was happy.

"It's a good opportunity for her. Could open more doors," Arthur said.

"She's very talented." Harrison fiddled with his car keys. "I hope things are okay between you guys."

Marci patted her hair. "I wish Penny had felt comfortable coming to us in the first place, but we've talked things out."

"Penny really loves you both," he said. "She sometimes feels like she doesn't measure up."

Arthur grimaced. "I think she takes things too seriously."

"She's a sensitive soul," Marci said. "I think it will take time, but our relationship is better."

The conversation waned and the silence grew awkward. Harrison glanced at the clock. "Listen, I'm sorry things went down the way they did. Penny and I—well we never meant to hurt anyone."

"We're not the ones who are hurting," Marci said quietly.

"You should go talk to her." Arthur's gaze flickered to Marci. "She needs to get things settled."

Settled. As in, get on with the divorce so this mistake can go away. Harrison's heart sank. Maybe he should go home and have his attorney draw up the papers so he could send them in the mail. Seeing her in person might not be the best idea.

Marci stood and walked over to him and placed her hand on his. "She needs to talk to you."

He swallowed, his heart in his throat. "Okay."

He was going to have to face Penny, no matter what she had to say.

CHAPTER 27

Penny finished the final notes of the song and the crowd exploded in applause. She let the feeling wash over her. There was nothing like performing. This was what she was born to do.

She gripped the microphone and looked out over the sea of faces in the crowd. Why was she looking for him? It was ridiculous, but she did it anyway. After each show. A face caught her attention and she sucked in a breath. That one really did look like him. She glanced away, the pain in her chest growing. It couldn't be him. Why did she torture herself?

The lights went out and she followed the backup singers. Holding up her shimmering evening gown, she tried not to trip, her fingers trembling. She needed to forget about him.

"Great show, Penny." Angela grinned at her. "Just when I think you've outdone yourself, you go and get even better."

Penny looped her arm through Angela's and patted her hand. "You're sweet to say that."

"I mean it. You're going to be a star someday."

"Just like you." Penny smiled at Angela. The girl had a lot of talent. If only she had the confidence to go with it.

Angela lowered her head and blushed.

Penny made her way to her dressing room. This was the part of the day she hated most. The part where she had to go home alone and face her life without him. She sat down at the mirror and began taking the pins out of her wig. She lifted the heavy thing off and combed through her hair.

A knock sounded on her door and Anthony poked his head in. "Hey, I've got a guy here claiming to be your husband. Should I have security toss him?"

Her heart jumped into her throat and she stood so fast her stool toppled over. "No!"

"No?" Anthony cocked his head to the side and lowered his clipboard. "You're married?"

"Yes. I mean, sort of. You can bring him back here." Her pulse raced. That *had* been Harrison in the audience. He'd come to watch her show. And now...what did he want with her?

She held her breath as the seconds ticked by. Was he here about the divorce? That had to be it, right? She gripped her dress and waited.

Harrison stepped into her dressing room and her mouth went dry. He wore a suit and tie, and he looked amazing. More than amazing. He was melt-you-with-a-glance gorgeous. All the feelings for him she'd tried to bury came back to her in a rush, leaving her speechless.

He shoved his hands in his pockets. "Hi."

She knew she had to speak to him, but words didn't want to come out. All this time away from him, wishing he were here, and now he stood before her and she couldn't talk. Great. She was toast. "Hi," she managed to croak.

"I...uh...your mom told me the show had opened up again."

"You called my mom?"

He looked down at his shoes. "I went to your house. I thought you were…still there."

Of course. He was looking for her so they could finalize the divorce. "Sorry. I should have told you I'd moved."

"I could have called."

Penny had thought about picking up the phone and dialing Harrison so many times. She'd even started to, but always lost the nerve. What would she have said? 'Even though we were strangers when we married, I fell in love with you over a two-week period, and now I want to have your babies?'

Harrison shifted his weight and glanced around her dressing room. "Nice."

"Thanks." His gaze landed on her fruit basket and she pointed. "Do you want an apple?"

He chuckled. "No, thanks."

"Do you mind if I have one? I'm starving."

Harrison waved his approval.

She plucked one out of the basket and took a bite. The fruit was a sweet distraction from the hurricane of feelings whipping around inside of her. She chewed and stared at him, waiting for him to get to the point.

Harrison scratched his chin. "Listen, I don't want to keep you. I just—" He stopped when his gaze landed on the cheap aluminum ring still on her wedding finger. "You're still wearing it."

She took a huge bite of her apple in an attempt not to have to answer him. Juice ran down her chin and she felt like a cow trying to chew such a large chunk. She wiped the juice as inconspicuously as she could and nodded.

He took a step toward her, and her heart went into overdrive. She didn't want him close to her. She couldn't handle that. She backed up against the table, but he kept advancing.

"Why are you still wearing that ring?" His intense blue eyes captured her gaze and wouldn't let go.

Her mouth was still full, and she tried to motion to him that she couldn't speak but ended up looking lame instead.

He captured her wrist and took the apple from her. He tossed it on the floor behind him and took another step closer to her. She could feel his breath on her cheek.

He reached up and brushed her hair from her face. "Penny, when we got married, I thought you were a means to an end. A way to get my money, and that's it. I never imagined I'd start to have feelings for you."

Did he just say he had feelings for her? Oh, why had she taken that big bite? She couldn't even respond. All she could do was chew as fast as she could and try not to choke.

"And I never imagined I'd fall in love with you."

She swallowed the rest in one gulp. What did he say? Her whole body buzzed with electricity. "You…you what?"

A smile tugged at his lips. "These past two months apart have been torture. I haven't been able to stop thinking about you, and now I realize I don't want to. I don't want to spend another minute apart."

He loved her. He'd come here to tell her. Her head spun and she tried to speak, but no words would come out. This was what she'd been dreaming about, and here he was. She refrained from pinching him to make sure he was real.

He reached into his pocket and pulled out a ring, then got down on one knee. "Penny, I love you with all my heart. I could not stand it if I lost you. Will you wear this ring, and stay with me forever?"

Tears welled in her eyes. "I will."

Harrison stood and wrapped her in an embrace. His lips brushed hers and she pulled him closer. "I've missed you so much," she said between kisses.

"I should never have left you." He slipped the cheap metal

band off her finger and replaced it with the beautiful diamond ring. "I've been carrying this around with me since we went to the mall."

Joy filled her and burst out of her in a laugh. "I think I've been in love with you ever since you put on that costume and took me to ElfCon. You looked so uncomfortable." She sobered. "But you did it for me."

He chuckled and lifted her chin so he could kiss her some more. "I was a goner the second you plastered your lips on mine in front of Josephine."

Her heart raced as he held her, and she placed her cheek on his chest. The feelings she had overwhelmed her, and she closed her eyes to soak in the moment.

"I have something I need to tell you."

She pulled back to look at him.

He seemed worried.

"What is it?"

"I told you Patrice handed over the trust account. What I didn't say was that there's only twenty-five thousand dollars in it."

She reached up and touched his cheek. "You must be so disappointed."

Harrison studied her for a moment. "I was furious when I first found out. I wanted to kill Patrice for what she did. But I've come to terms with it."

Penny smiled up at him. "You're beautiful, inside and out."

"Beautiful, huh?" He wiggled his eyebrows up and down and she laughed out loud. "I do have some better news."

"Go on."

"I'm done at the firm. Trent's taking over." He paused. "And I'm opening up a restaurant."

Penny squealed and hugged him. "That's great!"

"I thought I could start looking at locations this weekend."

"Here?"

A smile took over his face. "Of course. The only downside I see is I'll have to compete with Lord of the Onion Rings."

Penny's laughter filled the room.

~

"Maybe we can just write her a letter." Penny shot him a nervous grin as they approached his stepmother's front door.

He couldn't help but chuckle. "No, we have to tell her in person."

"Okay, as long as we're out of range."

He quirked an eyebrow at her.

"You know, stabbing range, punching range…"

It felt good to laugh with Penny. It actually felt amazing to be by her side, walking together as husband and wife. They'd snuck away over the past three days and had an incredible secret honeymoon in Puerto Rico. It had been private, and intimate, and his heart swelled with love for her.

He opened the door and led her down the marble hallway. The pristine house seemed so sterile. There was no warmth. Funny, he'd never felt it before.

Their footsteps echoed as they walked down the hall and Patrice came out to see who was making noise. "Oh. It's you." Patrice looked down her nose at Penny.

Harrison grasped Penny's hand. "Penny and I are staying married." He knew his declaration wouldn't be met with approval, but he didn't care. It was time to get out from under her thumb.

His stepmother fingered her pearls and looked Penny up and down. "I see." She frowned at him, but then motioned to the other room. "Why don't we go sit? I was just about to have some tea."

An invitation to tea was not what he was expecting. He looked at Penny, who nodded. "Okay, then."

Patrice waltzed into the sitting room and picked up a tea kettle. She poured a cup and offered it to Penny. Harrison wasn't about to ask her why she was pouring her own tea. She must have cut back on some of the staff.

Penny took the cup and sat down. "Thank you."

Harrison sat next to Penny and put his arm around her. When his stepmother offered him a cup, he shook his head. "No, thank you."

Patrice frowned but sat in her chair and crossed her ankles. She assessed them. "I take it there's some mutual benefit to this relationship."

"We're in love," Harrison said.

A grimace appeared on her face before she gained control and smoothed it away. She lifted her cup to her lips and took a sip. After she set her cup down, she cleared her throat. "I'm not sure it's wise to—"

"It's not up for discussion," Harrison interrupted her. "We're simply informing you."

Penny cast him a worried glance and took several large gulps of her tea, draining the cup.

"I see." Patrice smoothed her dress. "Anything else?"

"Trent's taking over the firm. I'm moving to Las Vegas with Penny." He had trouble making the last part come out. "I'm opening a restaurant."

Patrice looked like she'd swallowed a mouthful of toilet water. "Of course you are. With no regard for the firm and what's best for this family."

"The firm is in good hands. And what's best for *my* family…" He took Penny's hand and squeezed it. "Is up to me and my wife."

Patrice's cheeks grew red and she looked like she would explode. "You will not disrespect—"

Penny shot up out of the seat. "He is not disrespecting you! Respect has to be *earned*. I can't believe you would want Harrison to be stuck in a job that doesn't offer him any happiness. He loves to cook, and he's darn good at it. He told me what you did for Antonio, and I admire that. You did a great thing. But I can't believe you would hide your relationship because of a perceived social status. So what if he's a chauffeur? People will get over it, and you'll be happy together. If you truly love him, you'd do what would make him happiest."

Penny stopped talking and stood there, her eyes wide as if she hadn't meant to say all that. Harrison stood up as well. "I think we're probably done here."

Patrice blinked and turned a darker shade of red. "I think we are." She stood, turned on her heel, and left the room.

Harrison let out a breath. "Well, that went better than I expected."

"I can't believe I said that." Penny covered her mouth with her hand.

He chuckled. "I'm proud of you. It needed saying."

"I don't know. It felt awfully good coming out, but I still probably shouldn't have said it."

He wrapped his arms around her and pulled her close, the warmth of her skin sending his heartbeat into overdrive. "Even after all she's done to you, you still care enough to say something. You are an amazing woman. I can't begin to tell you how much you mean to me. You—"

She silenced him with a kiss.

EPILOGUE

Penny snuggled her back into Harrison's chest as she stretched out on the couch. This was the time of day she loved the most. The right-before-bed lazy time where she and Harrison could sit and watch television together and be close. He wrapped his arms around her.

"How was your day?" His deep voice made her heart flutter.

"Busy, with the dental appointment and the promotional shoot for my show." She still had trouble believing it. Her very own Las Vegas show, with her name on it. It was amazing. "How about you?"

He ran his fingers up her arm and tingles shot over her skin. "A little stressful. We got word that Phillip Irving was going to be in the restaurant today."

She turned to look at him. "The food critic?"

"Yes. The staff got all worked up."

"The staff did, huh?" She grinned.

He chuckled. "Okay, maybe I was a bit nervous, too."

"Did he come in?"

"He must have. No one knows what he looks like, of

course, but this appeared on his blog this evening." Harrison handed her his phone and she scrolled through the article.

"Aw, he loved it! That's so great, honey." She twisted to give him a peck on the lips, which lingered and turned into a deeper kiss. Her pulse quickened as the kiss grew more passionate.

He pulled back and placed his forehead on hers. "I missed you today."

She held in a smile. He told her that every day. "I missed you, too."

"You know, if you quit your job, you could come work for me. You'd be an amazing bookkeeper. You wouldn't need a calculator."

"As if." She playfully whacked him. "Like I'd give up a singing gig to do math all day." She made a face.

He reached behind his back and pulled a piece of paper out. "This came today."

She took it from him and stared at it. "A check? Holy cow, that's a lot of money."

"Trent says it's back pay for all the time I worked at the firm without taking a draw."

She whistled. "They must be doing well, then."

"Trent pulled the company around. They're seeing phenomenal numbers." He began running his fingers up her arm again, and she giggled.

"You're distracting me."

"Good." His breath tickled her ear.

"I bet Patrice is thrilled."

"She is. But I actually think she's more relieved that Antonio is finally cancer free."

"I'm still shocked they got married."

He chuckled. "Even a secret wedding is a step in the right direction, huh?"

She waved the check. "So what're we going to do with the money?"

He took her hand and entwined his fingers with hers. "I don't know. I thought maybe we could look for a bigger house."

They'd been living in a small two bedroom home for a couple of years now. It was modest and affordable, and she'd thought they had plenty of room. "Why? We don't need anything fancy."

"I know. I just thought maybe it was time to think about expanding our family." He placed his warm hand on her belly.

They'd talked about having kids a few times, but Harrison had always wanted to wait until his restaurant was more established. An excited flutter went through her. "Now?"

He grinned that sexy smile of his. "Yes. I think it's time."

She squealed and wrapped her arms around his neck, kissing him again. She'd wanted to start a family right away. She felt strongly that having children was important. And now that his restaurant was doing well and her singing career was stable, they could juggle her show schedule to make it work. "That's great news."

"In fact." He wiggled his eyebrows. "We should probably get started on that right away."

She laughed. "Oh, you think so?"

"I do." He kissed her again, and she ran her fingers up through his hair. He silenced the television and then reached over and clicked off the Elvis lamp, bathing the room in darkness.

Funny how the biggest mistake of her life turned out to be the best thing that ever could have happened to her.

The End

AFTERWORD

Thank you for reading! If you like Victorine's books, check out her bundles she has on sale on her website. You can save big with a bundle! Use the code 20OFF and get 20% off your entire order!

www.victorinelieske.com

If you want to read what Victorine is writing as she writes it, check out her Patreon. For just a few bucks a month you can get early access to her stories!: https://www.patreon.com/Victorine

Join Victorine's Newsletter and get a free novella: Her Sister's Fiancé. https://BookHip.com/CXNTMH

VICTORINE'S T-SHIRT SHOP

Sometimes the characters in Victorine's novels wear funny t-shirts. If you like them, you can buy them at Victorine's T-shirt shop.

And it's not just T-shirts, Victorine has cloth masks, mugs, and other merchandise. They're fun! Take a peek!

https://victorinelieske.threadless.com/

ABOUT THE AUTHOR

Victorine and her husband live in Nebraska with their four children and two cats. She loves all things romance, and is currently addicted to Korean Dramas, which are super swoony and romantic. (She highly recommends Crash Landing on You on Netflix.)

When she's not writing, she's designing book covers for authors or making something with her extensive yarn collection.

Made in United States
Cleveland, OH
25 May 2025